"Our fights always ended this way..."

The husky note of desire in Wade's voice made Maggie suddenly forget all their angry words. She was swept back into the past, before the divorce, when loving Wade had been as natural as disagreeing with him.

When he took her into his arms and kissed her, she was filled with happiness—and hope. Perhaps they could start again. Perhaps Wade wanted a reconciliation!

He released her abruptly. "Old habits die hard, don't they?" he mused, his gaze lingering on her face. "But now that we've stopped arguing, I'll tell you what I really came to say."

Wade paused, a muscle twitching along his jaw. "Congratulations are in order, Maggie. I'm getting married again."

JANET DAILEY AMERICANA

ALABAMA—Dangerous Masquerade
ALASKA—Northern Magic
ARIZONA—Sonora Sundown
ARKANSAS—Valley of the Vapours
CALIFORNIA—Fire and Ice
COLORADO—After the Storm
CONNECTICUT—Difficult Decision
DELAWARE—The Matchmakers
FLORIDA—Southern Nights
GEORGIA—Night of the Cotillion
HAWAII—Kona Winds
IDAHO—The Travelling Kind
ILLINOIS—A Lyon's Share
INDIANA—The Indy Man
IOWA—The Homeplace
KANSAS—The Mating Season
KENTUCKY—Bluegrass King
LOUISIANA—The Bride of the Delta Queen
MAINE—Summer Mahogany
MARYLAND—Bed of Grass
MASSACHUSETTS—That Boston Man
MICHIGAN—Enemy in Camp
MINNESOTA—Giant of Mesabi
MISSISSIPPI—A Tradition of Pride
MISSOURI—Show Me

MONTANA—Big Sky Country
NEBRASKA—Boss Man from Ogallala
NEVADA—Reilly's Woman
NEW HAMPSHIRE—Heart of Stone
NEW JERSEY—One of the Boys
NEW MEXICO—Land of Enchantment
NEW YORK—Beware of the Stranger
NORTH CAROLINA—That Carolina Summer
NORTH DAKOTA—Lord of the High Lonesome
OHIO—The Widow and the Wastrel
OKLAHOMA—Six White Horses
OREGON—To Tell the Truth
PENNSYLVANIA—The Thawing of Mara
RHODE ISLAND—Strange Bedfellow
SOUTH CAROLINA—Low Country Liar
SOUTH DAKOTA—Dakota Dreamin'
TENNESSEE—Sentimental Journey
TEXAS—Savage Land
UTAH—A Land Called Deseret
VERMONT—Green Mountain Man
VIRGINIA—Tide Water Lover
WASHINGTON—For Mike's Sake
WEST VIRGINIA—Wild and Wonderful
WISCONSIN—With a Little Luck
WYOMING—Darling Jenny

Janet Dailey
Americana

FOR MIKE'S SAKE

Harlequin Books

TORONTO • NEW YORK • LONDON
AMSTERDAM • PARIS • SYDNEY • HAMBURG
STOCKHOLM • ATHENS • TOKYO • MILAN
MADRID • WARSAW • BUDAPEST • AUCKLAND

The state flower depicted on the cover of this book is western rhododendron.

Janet Dailey Americana edition published May 1988
Second printing November 1988
Third printing November 1989
Fourth printing November 1990
Fifth printing January 1992
Sixth printing October 1992
Seventh printing January 1993

ISBN 0-373-89897-5

Harlequin Presents edition published October 1979
Second printing February 1982

Original hardcover edition published in 1979
by Mills & Boon Limited

FOR MIKE'S SAKE

CHAPTER ONE

THE COMPACT CONVERTIBLE zipped down the street, trees leafed out into full foliage to shade the lawns on either side.

The car's top was down, wind ruffling the scarlet gold hair of the driver, dressed in snug fitting Levi's and a blue madras blouse with the sleeves rolled up to the elbows.

Expertly shifting down to make a running stop at an intersection, Maggie Rafferty saw no traffic approaching and let the little car dart across. Ahead was the ball park and Maggie slowed the car to turn into the small graveled lot near the stand.

Stopped, she lifted the smoke gray sunglasses from her nose and perched them on her head. Her green eyes scanned the cluster of young boys as she pressed a hand on the horn.

Instantly one separated himself from the others and ran toward her, a baseball glove in his hand.

He paused once to wave at the group, backpedaling toward the car.

"See ya Friday, guys!" When he hopped into the passenger seat he was faintly breathless, his dark eyes glittering with excitement. "Hi!"

"Hi, yourself." Maggie smiled, tiny dimples appearing in her cheeks. "Sorry I'm late. I hope you didn't have to wait too long."

"That's okay." He shrugged away the apology, absently punching a fist into his glove. "I'm getting used to you always being late," he said with the patient indulgence of an adult.

"Thanks a lot, Mike." She laughed and reached over to tug the bill of his baseball cap low on his forehead.

Punctuality had never been one of her virtues, but she didn't need a ten-year-old son reminding her of it.

"Hey, come on!"

Mike protested the action, removing his cap and putting it back on at the correct angle. Its momentary removal revealed coal black hair, a shade darker than his eyes.

Maggie's gaze skimmed his profile, lighting on the sprinkling of freckles across the bridge of his nose. They were the only thing he might have inherited from her. "I told you not to do that."

"Sorry, I forgot." Which wasn't totally true. Mike believed himself to be too old for hugging and kissing. It embarrassed him.

Maggie couldn't smother the urge to touch him and love him, so she hid it under the guise of teasing pokes and gestures.

"Are we going home or not?" he prompted.

"Yes, right now."

As she turned toward the door to look over her shoulder for traffic before reversing into the street, Maggie's gaze was caught by the man standing on the driver's side of a station wagon parked beside her.

Tall, in his thirties, with light brown hair and hazel eyes, he was very good-looking, as suntanned as a lifeguard.

The look in his eyes was decidedly admiring in his inspection of her. His mouth quirked into a smile, accompanied by a slight nod of his head in silent greeting.

Maggie returned the smile and the nod without hesitation. One of Mike's teammates raced around the station wagon to climb in the passenger seat, and Maggie breathed out a sigh of regret. Why were the good-looking ones always married with a little wife waiting at home?

She flipped the sunglasses down on her nose and reversed into the empty street.

"How was your first practice?" The Little League baseball season was just beginning. Maggie didn't want to think about the hectic summer schedule that would be ahead.

"Great. The coach says I'm going to make a good utility man, 'cause I can play any position on the field . . . except pitcher, of course. Maybe I should practice pitching."

He considered the idea.

"Instead of being good at every position, you should concentrate on one or two and become the best at those."

"I guess," Mike conceded.

"I've gotta improve on my hitting. I didn't do too well today."

"It's only your first practice," Maggie reminded him.

"Yeah, I know. Coach said he'd give me a few pointers about switch-hitting and all if I'd come earlier than the other guys for practice. Do you suppose you could manage to bring me early?''

"You wouldn't have been late today if Aaron hadn't called from the office just as we were leaving." Maggie correctly interpreted the question as a slur on her character.

"Yeah, but you always leave everything to the last minute. Then when something comes up, we're always late.''

"We'll get an earlier start next time," she promised.

There was a flash of blue at the end of a side street, the shimmer of sunlight off the smooth surface of water.

In Seattle there always seemed to be a flash of blue around the corner, whether from a lake or an inlet or Puget Sound itself.

"You don't have to take me. I could always walk.''

"We've been through that before, Mike." Her mouth was set in a firm line, irritation sparking through her that he should bring up the subject when she had made her feelings so plain on it before. "It's too far for you to walk.''

"It wouldn't be too far if I had a bike, a ten-speed. I saw one the—"

"Your birthday is coming up.''

Mike groaned.

"Summer will almost be over by then!''

"If you'd taken better care of your old bike, you wouldn't be without one now.''

"I only forgot to lock it that one time. How was I supposed to know someone was going to come along and steal it?''

"I hope it taught you a lesson and you'll be more careful with your next bike."

"If you're going to get me a bike for my birthday, do I have to wait clear till then? Couldn't I have it early?"

"We'll see."

"Maybe if I wrote dad, he'd buy me one now," he muttered, not content with her half promise.

Maggie gave him an angry sidelong look.

"You just ruined your chances of getting a bike before your birthday. I've told you repeatedly that you aren't going to play me and your father off against each other. If you persuade him to buy you a bike before your birthday, I'll lock it up until your birthday. Do you understand?"

"Yes, ma'am," Mike grumbled, hanging his head, his mouth thinning into a sulking pout.

Concealing a sigh, Maggie let her green eyes look back to the road. God, how she hated playing the heavy-handed parent!

But she had little choice, really. Mike was only behaving as any child of divorced parents would. If she let him get away with his emotional blackmail, he'd be walking all over her. And *nobody* walked over her, certainly not her own son.

"It isn't so bad, is it?" she asked, trying to ease the friction between them. "To have me take you to practice?"

"No, it isn't so bad," he agreed glumly.

"From now on, I'll make sure you're there early so the coach can give you some tips on hitting, okay?"

"Okay."

As she glanced at him, Mike gave her a sideways

look through thick black lashes. A sudden, impish light glittered in his dark eyes. "I know why you're going to get me there early. It's the coach, isn't it?"

One thing about Mike, he never held a grudge, a trait that was totally his own.

Maggie smiled. "The coach?" She didn't follow his comment.

"Yeah, the coach." There was a knowing grin on his face. "I saw the way he looked at you."

"The way he looked at me?" She laughed in bewilderment. "I don't know what you're talking about. I didn't even see Coach Anderson at the ball park."

"He isn't our coach this year. We've got a new one, Tom Darby."

"Oh," said Maggie in understanding and repeated the sound in realization. "Oh, your new coach was the one by the station wagon, the tall, good-looking man."

"Yeah, do you want me to introduce you?"

His dark eyes were twinkling with an awareness beyond his years, but then children seemed to grow up quicker nowadays.

Maggie hid a smile at his matchmaking attempt, but there were telltale dimples in her cheeks despite the straight line of her mouth.

"The coach's wife just might object to that, Mike."

"He isn't married."

His grin deepened.

"The boy who got into the station wagon with him . . . ."

" . . . was Ronnie Schneider. Coach was giving him a ride home. You don't think I'd try to line you up with a guy who's married and has kids of his own, do you, mom?''

"You can just forget about lining me up with him. If there's any lining up to do, I'll take care of it." As they turned a corner the wind blew her hair across her cheek, flame silk against her ivory complexion. Maggie pushed the tangling strands back.

"From the look he gave you, it won't take much lining up," Mike declared with decided certainty. "He'd like to make it with you—I could tell."

His candor brought a bubble of indignant reproof, but Maggie swallowed back most of it, releasing a tame reprimand.

"You see more than you should."

"It's a fact of life, mom. A feller can't ignore it." He shrugged, knowing he was being outrageous and enjoying the feeling.

"It's not my fault I have a beautiful mother and that half the guys think you're my older sister."

"Do you mind?"

She slid him a curious glance as she turned the car into the driveway of their home.

"Nah, I just tell everybody that you had a face-lift and you're really a lot older."

"Mike!"

She didn't know whether to be angry or laugh, and in the confusion became capable of neither.

He laughed heartily, finding her astonishment riotously funny.

"I don't tell them that, mom, honest. But you should have seen the look on your face!"

Maggie stopped the car in front of the garage door.

"Wait until you see the look on your face if I ever find out that you have!"

But the threat wasn't made in earnest.

"Seriously, mom—" he opened the door and hesitated before stepping out of the small car "—I don't mind that you look young and beautiful. And I wouldn't mind a bit if the coach was your boyfriend."

"Oh, you wouldn't?"

Maggie switched off the engine and removed the key from the ignition. "Do you think it might help you to score a few points with the coach?"

"It couldn't hurt. It would be pretty hard for him to bench the son of the girl he's dating, wouldn't it?"

"If you deserve benching, the mother might suggest it to the coach."

"Oh, well," he sighed as he climbed out of the car, "you can't blame a guy for trying to cover all the angles if he can."

With a shake of her head, Maggie stepped onto the concrete driveway. Mike took the short flight of steps to the front door two at a time and waited impatiently at the top while Maggie rummaged through her cloth purse for the house key.

"What's for lunch? I'm starved!"

"Homemade noodles." She handed him the key to unlock the door and reached for the letters in the mailbox.

"Can we eat now?"

He was in the house, tossing his baseball glove on the sofa while he headed for the kitchen.

"The glove belongs in your room and we'll eat in twenty minutes, after you've washed and I've fixed a salad."

"You're trying to turn me into a rabbit. Salad!" Mike declared.

"The glove and wash," Maggie reminded him, catching him before he reached the kitchen and turning him back to the living room. "And you like salad, so I don't know why you're complaining about it now."

"I don't like it for every meal."

As Mike retraced his path to the living room, Maggie had to admit her menus had been lacking in imagination lately.

She supposed it was a problem all working mothers faced. Cooking for only two people wasn't easy, either.

Still, Mike's criticism was justified and she should do something about changing it in what was left of her two weeks' vacation.

Maggie set the mail on the counter and began rummaging through the kitchen cupboards. There would be time enough to look over the bills later. Right now, she had a hungry boy to feed.

Boy. Dimples were carved briefly in her cheeks at the word. After that observation about his coach, Mike was fast outgrowing the term of *boy*.

And matchmaking yet. Still, it was better that he had no objections to her dating. It would have been unbearable if he were jealous and resentful of her seeing other men.

But Mike had only been five years old when Maggie had finally obtained her divorce, so his emotional scars were few.

Mike evidently liked his new coach. Tom Darby—Maggie remembered the name.

He was good-looking, in a jock sort of way, and she

would have been less than honest if she didn't admit that she had been attracted to him. He evidently liked children, otherwise he wouldn't be coaching a boys' Little League team.

Most of the eligible men she had met lately had either been too young or too old, but this Tom Darby was . . . . Maggie took a firm grip on her imagination. The man hadn't even asked her out yet—if he ever would—and here she was assessing his possibilities!

Mike burst into the kitchen.

"My glove's in my room and my hands are washed. Can we eat now?"

Maggie made a brief inspection of him and nodded. "Set the table while I see what I can fix in place of a salad."

"Can't we just forget the salad? I promise I'll eat two helpings of green vegetables at dinner tonight instead. I'm starved! I really worked up an appetite at the ball field."

She smiled crookedly and gave in.

"All right, set the table and I'll dish up the beef and noodles."

Later when Mike helped himself to another portion of noodles, Maggie carried her empty plate to the sink, picked up the mail from the counter and returned to the table.

She sifted through the half-dozen envelopes, a mixture of advertisements and billing statements, until she came to the last.

Even before she saw the Alaskan postmark, she recognized the boldly legible handwriting. Her heart missed a beat, then resumed its normal pace.

"You have a letter from your father, Mike."

Her thumb covered the return address and the name Wade Rafferty as Maggie handed the envelope to her son.

"Great!" He abandoned his plate to tear open the flap with the eagerness of a child opening a present. Maggie sipped at her glass of milk, trying to ignore her pangs of jealousy.

Mike read the first paragraph and exclaimed, "Oh, boy! He's coming home!"

Her heart missed another beat. "Why is he coming to Seattle?"

She refused to use the word *home*.

"To see us, of course." Mike continued to read the contents of the letter.

Not us. He's coming to see you, but not us, Maggie corrected him silently.

Wade had no more interest in seeing her than she had in seeing him.

"Does your father say when he's coming?"

It had been six years since she had seen him last, shortly after their divorce, before he'd left for Alaska, a transfer Wade had requested from his company. Of course Mike had seen him regularly, flying to Alaska in the summers and during Christmas holidays.

The first time Mike had gone, it had been awful, with Maggie worrying about him every second. But it had been even worse when he came back, every other sentence containing "daddy." Even today, she still experienced moments of jealousy, although none as intense as that first time.

To say her five-year marriage and year's separation

from Wade had been stormy was an understatement. It had been six years of one flaming argument after another, each alternately demanding a divorce from the other until finally their demands coincided.

They had been too much of a match for each other, her fiery temper equal to his black rage. Yet, since their divorce they had managed to be civil to each other for Mike's sake, albeit at long distance.

"He's coming home Sunday the . . . ." Mike glanced up at the calendar hanging on the kitchen wall, notes scribbled on various dates. "Wow! He's coming home *this* Sunday!"

He pointed at a section of the letter. "He says right here, 'I'll see you on Sunday. I'll call you first thing in the morning.' This Sunday. Wow!" Mike repeated with incredulity and delight.

"Does he say why? I mean, didn't you write him in your last letter and tell him how much you were looking forward to coming to Alaska this summer?" Maggie felt uneasy.

It was so much better when there were hundreds of miles separating her from Wade. "Surely your father knows how much you wanted to come, so why would he disappoint you this way?"

"I'm not disappointed. I'd much rather have him come here. Dad knows that, 'cause I keep asking him to come home. Mom, do you suppose he could—"

"He is not staying here!" She read the rest of the question in Mike's expression and immediately rejected the idea.

"And I'm sure your father wouldn't want to, anyway."

"It was just a thought." Mike shrugged and tried to hide his disappointment.

There was sudden perception in her green eyes as Maggie studied her son's face.

"Mike," she began hesitantly, "I hope you aren't holding out any hopes that your father and I will get back together again. We both tried very hard to make our marriage work, but we simply couldn't get along."

"Yeah, I know." He neither admitted nor denied that he had been hoping. "I remember the way you used to yell at each other. That's about all I can remember."

"I'm sorry, Mike."

He folded the letter back up and inserted it into its envelope.

"I hate fighting," he declared with unexpected vehemence.

Maggie's head lifted a fraction as she realized that Mike's unwillingness to argue or remain angry for long was a result of the shouting matches he had overheard. She and Wade had inflicted a few scars on him.

"Arguments can be good, Mike. They can clear the air, bring things out in the open and straighten out misunderstandings. It's normal for two people to argue. In the case of me and your father, we were simply never able to resolve our differences. We weren't able to reach a mutual understanding. Sometimes it happens that way." She tried to explain, but it was difficult.

"Weren't you ever happy with him?"

"Of course. In the very beginning," Maggie admitted. "Your father swept me off my feet in the true romantic fashion. He was very masterful. It wasn't until after we were married that I realized that I didn't want to be mastered. And your father couldn't regard me as an equal.''

Mike impatiently pushed his chair away from the table. "Why do you always have to refer to him as 'your father'? He has a name just like everybody else,'' he muttered.

"It's a habit, I suppose. Something that's carried over from the days when you were younger." That wasn't exactly the truth. It was still difficult for her to say Wade's name. To say "your father" came easier; Maggie couldn't explain why.

"Well, he's coming Sunday anyway, and I'm glad." Mike rose from his chair, ignoring the food on his plate. "I think I'll go see if Denny wants to play catch."

Again Maggie took note of the way he had avoided an argument with her.

It was his turn to do the dishes, but she didn't bother to remind him of it.

She'd do them this time.

AT THE NEXT PRACTICE SESSION Maggie kept her word and arrived at the ball park early so Mike could get the extra coaching on his hitting game. One of his young teammates was already there, sitting in the bleachers and tossing a ball in the air.

"There's Ronnie!"

Mike hopped from the car before Maggie could shift the gear into park. Closing the car door, he paused a second to ask, "Can you stay for a while to watch me practice?"

The station wagon Tom Darby had been driving the last time was nowhere to be seen. Maggie hesitated, then agreed.

"I'll stay, at least until your coach gets here."

Maggie stayed mostly because she didn't like the idea of leaving Mike alone—an overly protective attitude, but she admitted to that.

There was also the motivation, though, of wanting to see Tom Darby again. First impressions could be misleading. Perhaps on second meeting Maggie would find him less attractive.

"Great!" Mike responded to her decision and raced off to greet his teammate.

Maggie followed at a more sedate pace.

By the time she reached the tall wire fence protecting spectators from the batting area of the diamond, Mike had persuaded the second boy to join him on the field. Maggie leaned a shoulder against a supporting post and watched them tossing the ball back and forth.

A car door slammed and she glanced over her shoulder at the sound. A viridescent shimmer brightened her eyes as casual, effortless strides carried Mike's coach toward her.

He was good-looking, almost too good-looking, she decided, letting her attention shift back to the boys on the playing field.

"Good morning." His voice was pleasantly low as he stopped beside her.

With the greeting, Maggie let her gaze swerve to him. The hazel eyes regarding her so admiringly had definite gold flecks. On closer inspection, her initial opinion didn't change.

"Good morning," she replied naturally. "It's a beautiful day, isn't it?"

He nodded agreement and added, "The kind of day Seattle people always brag about, but seldom see."

Maggie didn't argue that the perfection of their weather was occasionally overstated. Instead she let her smile widen and remarked, in question form, "You aren't from around here, then?"

"No, not originally. I'm a native southern Californian."

It fitted. With that deep golden tan, he looked as if he had walked straight off the beach. "But I'm beginning to enjoy the change of scenery."

The lazily explicit way he was eyeing her plainly indi-cated that he wasn't referring to the landscape of mountains and sea. No woman with an ounce of femininity could be immune to that look.

Certainly Maggie wasn't. If she had possessed any doubt that she was a strikingly attractive woman, it no longer existed.

"It's a nice place to live." Her noncommittal reply didn't reveal that she had interpreted a second meaning to his remark.

Her gaze shifted back to the baseball diamond and the two boys. As yet, neither had noticed the arrival of their coach.

And Tom Darby was in no hurry to make them aware of his presence. That fact produced a warm glow of satisfaction in Maggie.

"Are you staying to watch the practice?" The way Tom asked the question seemed to imply that he would like it if she did.

"I'm afraid I can't." A rueful smile tugged at one corner of her mouth. "I have a bunch of errands to do this morning. I promised Mike I'd only stay for a few minutes.''

Maggie didn't tell him that she had agreed to wait only until he came.

She didn't want him to think he had been the sole reason, or even the main reason she had waited, because it wasn't so.

At the same time she didn't want to totally rebuff the interest he was showing in her.

This time Tom was the one to glance at the two boys playing catch. "Your little brother is a very good ball player."

"He isn't my brother," Maggie corrected him with a laughing gleam in her green eyes.

"Mike is my son."

Startled hazel eyes flicked a surprised look back to her. "I beg your pardon, Mrs. Rafferty. You must have been a child bride."

"No, I wasn't. And the name is Maggie."

"Tom Darby," he introduced himself, his gaze sliding to her ringless left hand.

Maggie saw the question forming in his expression and was about to inform him of her unattached status when a shout of recognition from Mike eliminated the chance.

Both boys came racing to the wire fence.

"You said if we came early, coach, you'd give us some tips on switch-hitting," Mike reminded him on a breathless note, all eagerness and enthusiasm.

"So I did," Tom smiled indulgently.

"The bats are in the back of my wagon. Why don't you two go get them?"

As they started to dash off to do his bidding, he called them to a halt.

"Wait a minute—it's locked. I'll have to get them for you."

The opportunity for private conversation was gone.

But Maggie wasn't concerned. There would be others.

"I'd better be going," she told everyone in general, but Tom in particular, as she started for her own car. Her parting remark was directed at her son. "I'll pick you up after practice."

"Okay."

He absently waved a goodbye.

THERE WASN'T ANOTHER CHANCE that week for the personal discussion the boys had interrupted. That day Maggie was late getting back to the ball park to pick up Mike, and Tom Darby had already left. At Mike's next practice Maggie brought him early but couldn't stay, and again picked him up late.

It couldn't be helped.

There was so much she wanted done before Wade returned this Sunday. The biggest task was spring-cleaning the house from top to bottom. She intended it to be spotless when he came.

Plus, there was shopping to be done for new kitchen and dining-room curtains. A new outfit in a shop window caught her eye and Maggie bought it, as well. Amid all the preparation, she squeezed in a visit to the beauty salon.

She was perfectly aware that she was doing all this because of Wade.

It was deliberate, if a trifle vindictive. She wanted him to see how very well she managed on her own. She was doing it all to impress him and wasn't ashamed to admit it to herself.

CHAPTER TWO

"HEY, MOM, are you going to sleep all morning? I'm hungry!"

Maggie opened one eye to see Mike standing in the doorway of her bedroom.

She groaned and pulled the covers over her head, trying to shut out her son and the daylight streaming through the window.

"Get yourself some cereal," she mumbled. "You're old enough to get your own breakfast."

"It's Sunday," he protested.

Maggie groaned again. It had become a Sunday-morning ritual that breakfast was a special meal. No hot cereal and toast, nor a quickly fried egg on this day. No, it was pancakes with blueberry syrup and bacon, eaten at leisure with neither of them rushing off anywhere, not to school nor work.

"Come on, mom, get up," Mike insisted when she failed to show any signs of rising. "Dad's going to be calling anytime now."

That opened her eyes as the full significance of the day hit her like a dousing of cold water.

Maggie tossed the covers back and rolled over to sit on the edge of the bed.

She yawned and paused to rub the sleep from her

eyes. Mike was still at the door, as if he expected her to slide back under the covers any minute.

"All right, I'm up. Go and put on some coffee." Maggie waved him toward the kitchen. "I'll be right there."

Mike hesitated, then trotted off.

She slid her feet into a pair of furry slippers and padded to the clothes closet. Ignoring the new robe hanging inside, she removed a faded quilted one from the hook.

"Old Faithful" had seen better days.

A seam was ripped out under an arm. Two buttons were off on the bottom.

But it was as comfortable as a pair of old shoes, cozy and warm and dependable.

She touched an inspecting hand to her hair to be certain all the clips and hair rollers were in place.

Setting her hair had been a precaution to keep the attractive style she had got at the beauty parlor the previous morning.

Sometimes the thickness of her red gold hair refused to keep the discipline of a style after being slept on and Maggie hadn't wanted to take a chance this time.

As much tossing and turning as she had done last night trying to get to sleep, it had probably been a good thing she had taken steps to make sure her hair looked right this morning.

She hadn't been able to forget that Wade was coming. She kept trying to imagine how she would treat him, what her manner would be.

She couldn't make up her mind whether she would be cool and polite or indifferently friendly. How, exactly, did one treat an ex-husband?

Even now the answer eluded her.

At the door to the bathroom, she paused. Shrugging, she walked toward the kitchen.

There would be time enough to fix her hair and put on makeup after Wade had telephoned to say when he was coming.

The coffeepot was perking merrily in the kitchen. Maggie inhaled the aroma wistfully and took out the skillet to begin frying the bacon.

While it sizzled in the pan, she mixed up the pancakes and heated the griddle, putting Mike to work setting the table.

As she stole a sip of the freshly brewed coffee she had poured, she noticed the way Mike kept eyeing the telephone extension by the cupboards. She knew he was anxious to receive the phone call from his father, but made no comment.

When she put the food on the table, Mike didn't eat his favorite meal with his usual enthusiasm. He did more playing than eating, his gaze constantly straying to the telephone.

Half a pancake was drowning in blueberry syrup, slowly disintegrating under his pushing fork.

"There's more bacon." Maggie offered him the platter.

He shook his head in refusal.

"Why hasn't he called yet? He said in his letter he'd call Sunday morning."

"It's a little early." The wall clock indicated a few minutes after eight o'clock. "Maybe he thinks you're still sleeping."

"But he knows I'll be waiting for him to call."

"He also said he'd be arriving late last night. Maybe your father is sleeping late this morning," Maggie suggested.

"Him? Dad never sleeps late."

Mike dismissed that suggestion as unworthy of any consideration.

Maggie had to admit that Mike was probably right. Wade had always been a disgustingly early riser, constantly-chiding her for being such a sleepyhead. Wade had always been punctual, if not early, for appointments, while she had been habitually late.

There was a long list of differences between them and they had been a continual source of conflict during their marriage.

"You'd better eat that pancake before it turns into mush," Maggie advised.

She turned her mind from the long-ago problems that had been resolved by a divorce.

"I'm not hungry anymore." Mike pushed his plate back.

His dark eyes gazed at the beige phone as if willing it to ring.

"You've heard the old saying, haven't you, Mike? 'A watched pot never boils.' I think your telephone is turning into a watched pot that isn't going to ring. Why don't you see if the paperboy has brought the Sunday newspaper yet?"

When he hesitated, Maggie added, "You can hear the phone ring outside and it won't take you a minute."

"Okay," he agreed, but reluctantly.

As Mike walked to the side door, Maggie rose to begin clearing the table. Leaving the dirty dishes for the moment, she covered the butter tray and put it in the refrigerator.

The door closed behind Mike.

Blueberry syrup had trickled down the side of its container. She wiped away the sticky substance with a dishcloth from the sink and put the syrup jar in the refrigerator.

As she picked up the bottle of orange juice, the lid wasn't on tight and skittered off onto the floor. It rolled into the narrow slit between the refrigerator and the cabinet.

"Damn!" Maggie muttered beneath her breath, and stooped down.

She could see the lid in the shadowy aperture. Kneeling, she worked her hand into the slit, just barely, and tried to reach the lid.

Her fingertips touched the edge. She wiggled her arm a little farther inside and hooked a fingernail in the inner rim.

Slowly and carefully she pulled her arm, her hand, and the lid out.

"Hey, mom! Look who brought the paper!" Mike's excited voice cried.

Maggie was on her hands and knees, twisting her head to see the door open. "Dad drove in just as I went outside." Mike glanced upward at the tall, dark man who had followed him into the house. "I thought you were going to call first."

"I was," the familiar, deep-pitched voice answered. "Since you were expecting me anyway, I decided not to bother, so I came over instead." Eyes equally black as his hair looked at Maggie. "Hello, Maggie."

The room spun crazily for a moment. She was paralyzed, unable to move.

There was a familiar leap of her pulse as she stared up at him.

Wade looked achingly the same as when she had first seen him.

That shaggy black mane of hair, those virile, rugged features, that self-assured carriage, all made an impact on her.

A cream silk shirt was opened at the throat, hinting at the perfectly toned muscles of his chest and shoulders.

The long sleeves were rolled up almost to the elbows, a look indolently casual and relaxed.

A whole assortment of disturbing memories came rushing back.

Her flesh remembered the evocative caress of those large hands. The warm taste of his mouth was recalled by her lips and the male scent of his body was strong in her memory.

Her ears could hear the husky love words Wade used to murmur to her.

The look of him needed no recalling. He was there, standing in her kitchen, his dark eyes glinting with silent mockery.

There were dirty dishes on the table. Cooking smells were strong in the air, the room smelling of bacon, thanks to the skillet on the stove and the grease splattered over the enameled range top.

The place was a mess.

So was she, Maggie realized. There were curlers and hair clips in her hair. She wore no makeup, and the faded and tattered robe did nothing to improve her appearance. She must seem the caricature of a housewife in the morning.

This wasn't how she had planned it.

The house was to be spotless, her appearance immaculate. Her new outfit, the two precious hours at the beauty parlor, all to prove how beautiful she still was, had all gone for naught.

Bitter frustration sparked her highly combustible temper.

"Damn you, Wade Rafferty!" Maggie pushed herself to her feet, stepping on the hem of her robe and nearly tripping.

She threw the orange juice lid that she had struggled so hard to reach onto the floor in a fit of pique.

"You did this on purpose. You deliberately came here without calling just to make me look . . . . Only you could be that rude and inconsiderate! Get out of my house!"

She was so angry that she was almost choking on her tears.

During the course of her tirade, the glittering light of mockery left Wade's eyes.

They became an ominous, brooding black, narrowing into piercing slits. His mouth had hardened into a thin line, bringing a forbidding quality to his harshly masculine features.

His hand had remained on the back of Mike's neck in a gesture of affection, but Wade, and Maggie, were indifferent to the presence of their son.

Until he called attention to himself.

"How could you do it, mom?"

His wavering voice and stricken look quenched Maggie's fiery temper.

The damage was already done. Her angry outburst had spoiled Mike's reunion with his father and there wasn't anything she could say to make it right. Her fingers curled into the palms of her hands as she strived to obtain some measure of dignity.

"I would appreciate it if you would have Michael back home by ten this evening."

Without allowing Wade an opportunity to respond to her cool statement, Maggie walked from the kitchen, her head held high.

Her cheeks burned with the knowledge of the farcical picture she made, acting like a lady of the house and looking like a hag.

The first thing she did, upon reaching her bedroom, was take off her old, comfortable robe and jam it into the small wastebasket in her room. Then she began tugging the curlers and silver clips from her hair and flinging them on her dresser.

She didn't stop until the door slammed, indicating Wade and Mike had left.

Then she slumped onto her bed, burying her face in her hands.

There was bitter disappointment and frustration in her mouth.

Yesterday she had been positive Wade no longer had the power to incite her to anger. Yet, within five seconds after seeing him she had been screaming at him like a shrew.

Why, oh, why did he always manage to succeed in making her lose her temper? And in front of Mike, too. Maggie groaned in despair.

There was only one lesson to be learned from the incident. Things were just as volatile between them as they always had been. From now on she would have to be on her guard.

In the meantime, she still had the task of facing Mike when he returned tonight.

CHAPTER THREE

THAT EVENING Maggie sat with forced quietness in a living-room chair.

The house was once again spotlessly clean. Not a single dirty dish was in the sink, nor an ash in the ashtrays. Her makeup was on and there was hardly a hair out of place on her head.

She was wearing the elegant jersey pantsuit in lavender that she had purchased for the occasion. Except for the tightly clasped hands in her lap, she appeared calm and completely controlled.

A car pulled into the driveway and she unconsciously held her breath. She heard a car door slam shut, but only one door.

As the kitchen door opened, the car reversed out of the driveway. Maggie slowly began breathing again.

"Hello, Mike." Her greeting was determinedly bright as she rose to meet him.

She glanced pointedly behind him. "Didn't your father come in with you?"

"No. After the way you yelled at him this morning, did you really think he would?" He didn't quite meet her eyes, but there was no malice in his tone, only the hurt of disappointment.

"No, I guess I didn't," Maggie admitted. "I baked a

cake this afternoon—chocolate with chocolate frosting.
Would you like a piece?"

"No, thanks." Mike wandered into the room and
slumped into the twin of the chair Maggie had been sitting
in. "I'm not hungry."

"Did you and yo—Wade have a good time together
today? Where did you go?"

She longed to ask if Wade had made any reference to
her waspish outburst, but she doubted that he had. He had
always possessed much more control over himself than
she had.

"Yeah, we had fun." His shrug expressed disinterest in
being more explicit. "We went down to the harbor and
took a ferry to one of the islands."

"Did your fa—did Wade say how long he'd be staying
in Seattle?"

"No."

Mike was usually more talkative than this and Maggie
knew the reason for his brief responses. She took a deep
breath and plunged into an apology. "I'm sorry about this
morning, Mike. I really am."

"How could you do it?" He sounded both puzzled and
hurt. "Dad says hello and you start yelling at him. Why?
Do you hate him that much?"

"No, I don't hate him." Maggie denied that suggestion
and qualified it in her mind that the violent side of her
emotion toward Wade surfaced only at times of supreme
anger.

"I don't know how to explain it to you, Mike. Maybe
you'd have to be a girl to understand." She attempted a
teasing smile, but he wasn't put off by it. "It's been five
years since I saw . . . Wade."

"I know, and the minute you see him you start shouting."

"That's because I had curlers in my hair, no lipstick on, dirty dishes all over the table and I was wearing that horrible old robe. I didn't want him to see me like that. I wanted to be all dressed up with my hair fixed and everything.

"I was embarrassed and because I was embarrassed I became angry. It doesn't excuse what I did, but I hope you understand why."

He considered the explanation for a minute, then nodded uncertainly.

"Yeah, I guess I do."

"Wade has always had a talent for catching me at my worst. I should have remembered that and been prepared." The milk was spilled and Maggie refused to cry about it.

"Yeah, well, the next time you see dad—"

"I'll try to remember. And I'll also apologize." She'd do it for Mike's sake.

"Dad didn't come over deliberately just to catch you looking like that," Mike said, defending his father.

"I know that . . . now. He was anxious to see you, that's why he came first instead of calling. He misses you just as much as you miss him." Maggie didn't have any doubt about that.

"Which reminds me, what are you two planning for tomorrow?"

"Dad's busy all day tomorrow. He said there were some things he had to do."

"Oh." Maggie frowned. "I thought you'd be spending the day with him, or at least part of it."

"I'm not. Why?"

"Aaron called this afternoon and asked me to work tomorrow."

"But you're on vacation," Mike protested.

"I know, but Patty's sprained her ankle and can't come in. Since it's only for Monday, I told Aaron I could. I thought you'd be with Wade."

She did some quick thinking. "I'll call Denny's mother." Shelley Bixby lived next door and kept an eye on Mike while Maggie worked.

"But what about the game?"

Maggie started for the telephone and stopped. "What game?"

"My baseball game tomorrow afternoon. It starts at five and coach wants us to be there no later than four-thirty. You don't get home until after five. If I'm late, I'll probably have to sit on the bench the whole time. I won't even have a chance to play."

"Don't start thinking the worst. Since I'm supposed to be on vacation, I'll simply tell Aaron that I have to leave by four."

She picked up the telephone receiver. "It's a pity Denny isn't in Little League. Then Shelley could take you both."

"You won't forget to tell him, will you, mom? You won't be late coming home?" Mike repeated skeptically.

Maggie's fingers hovered above the telephone dial. "I won't forget, and I won't be late."

BUT SHE VERY NEARLY WAS.

She didn't leave the office until five past four the next day. A traffic light failed to function properly and there

was a snarl of cars at the major intersection where she had
to turn.

Five minutes before Mike had to be at the ball park, she
turned into the driveway and honked the horn. Mike was
waiting on the front doorstep and was halfway to the car
before she had stopped it.

He was wearing his striped baseball player's uniform,
complete with the billed cap, socks and shoes. He looked
cute, but he would have blushed scarlet if Maggie had told
him so.

Mike shot her an impatient glance as he hopped into the
passenger side of the car.

"You're late."

"Only a couple of minutes," Maggie hedged, and put
the car in reverse when his door was shut.

"Dad said I should set all our clocks ahead an hour and
then you'd be on time."

She felt a surge of anger at the unrequested suggestion,
but squelched it.

"I haven't been doing too badly."

Luckily there was little traffic to slow her up. Several
other parents were just arriving with their children when
she reached the ball park.

There was a faint smugness to the smile she gave
Mike.

"See? You aren't the last one here." She stopped the
car at the curb so he could get out.

He stood outside by the door. "Aren't you going to
watch me play?"

"You said the game didn't start until five. I'm going
home to change my clothes, then come back. This outfit—" Maggie touched the ivory material of her skirt and

its matching top ''—isn't what I want to wear if I have to sit in those dirty bleachers.''

''Okay. See you later.''

And Mike dashed off to where his team was congregating.

Maggie smiled wryly as she drove the car away from the curb.

At least he hadn't cautioned her not to be late. There were times when she wondered who was the parent and who was the child!

Parking the dark green compact in the driveway, she climbed out of the car and dug into her purse for the house key.

She unlocked the front door and held it open with her foot as she took the mail out of the box.

Once inside, she let the door shut on its own and walked into the living room.

She sifted quickly through the mail as she went, kicking her shoes off and letting her bag slide from her shoulder onto a chair.

Halfway to her bedroom, the doorbell rang.

Doing an about-face, Maggie walked back to answer it.

With a brief glance at her wristwatch, she opened the door and stopped dead.

It was Wade, and her heart fluttered madly against her ribs.

She had forgotten how overpowering he could be at close quarters.

Not because of his height, although he was tall. Her forehead came to the point of his chin and no higher. Nor because of his bulk, since his brawny shoulders and chest were in proportion to his frame. His hands were large and his fingers long, easily capable of spanning her waist.

No, the sensation was all wrapped up in the sheer force of his presence.

The years had made few changes, adding character lines to his sun- and snow-browned face. They hadn't blunted the angular thrust of his jaw nor softened his square chin.

There was a closed look to his Celtic black eyes, although the shutters could be thrown open at any time and they would be alive with expression.

The background of Alaska suited Wade, a land raw and untamed, demanding a man capable of compromising with the elements.

It required intelligence, keen insight, and a large measure of self-confidence.

Yet these were the very traits needed to succeed in a so-called civilized society. Wade could slip in or out of either world at will.

All these things were assimilated with the lightning swiftness of the mind.

Then Maggie noticed Wade had cocked his head slightly to one side.

She realized she had been staring and hadn't spoken a word of greeting.

The day's mail was still in her hand. She stood in her stockinged feet, her titian hair windblown, her makeup fading. Again Wade had appeared when she was less than her best.

She managed to curb part of the rush of irritation, but some of it slipped through to make her voice curt.

"Mike isn't here. He has a Little League ball game tonight."

"Aren't you going to watch him play? Children like to have their parents there, cheering them on."

Maggie bristled. "What is this? Are you trying to insinuate that I'm not a good mother to Mike? That I'm somehow neglecting him?"

"I merely asked a question." Wade elevated a dark brow. "I can't control the way your conscience interprets it."

"My conscience?" Maggie breathed in sharply at the inference of guilt. "What about yours? I've attended every function Mike has participated in. Can you say the same?"

"I never said that I could."

"Before you start throwing stones, you'd better check to see if your windows have shatterproof glass," she warned.

"I wasn't throwing stones. I asked a question that you still haven't answered."

"As a matter of fact, I am going to watch him play. I came home to change my clothes first. The game starts at five—" Maggie glanced at her watch, the seconds ticking away "—so I don't have time to argue with you.

"Instead of being so concerned about me, why don't you fulfill your duty as Mike's father and go to the game? It would be quite a novelty to Mike to have his father there for once."

"I've been planning to go to the game ever since Mike mentioned it to me yesterday."

"Then what are you doing here? Oh, of course, you don't know where the game is being played, do you?"

Sarcasm crept into her voice. She stepped onto the threshold to point out the direction, her arm brushing his shoulder.

"You go down to this next corner and turn—"

"I know where the ball park is," Wade interrupted.

"What's the point of coming here, then?" Maggie stepped back, the brief contact jolting through her like the charge of a lightning bolt.

"If it was just to make sure that I was going, you've wasted your time and mine."

"I wanted to speak to you privately, although preferably not on the doorstep."

He pointedly drew attention to the fact that she had not invited him in.

A different sort of tension raced through her nerve ends. "I can't think of a single thing we need to discuss, in private or otherwise."

"Mike."

Wade supplied the subject.

"Mike?"

Maggie stiffened. "He's doing just fine. He's healthy and active, as normal as any boy his age. Unless—" her worst fears surfaced "—you intend to sue for custody of him. I'll fight that, Wade. You won't take my son away from me.

"There isn't anything you could say that would persuade me differently."

His mouth quirked in a humorless smile.

"I wouldn't try. That would be like trying to take a cub away from a tigress. You can sheathe your claws, Maggie. I have no intention of trying to get custody of Mike."

She was confused, and still wary.

"Then why—"

"It's in Mike's interest that I want to speak to you. May I come in?"

He smiled a slow smile that melted most of her resistance despite her better judgment.

After a moment's hesitation she swung the door open wider and backed away from the opening to admit him.

With a briskness she was far from feeling she walked into the living room, pausing to pick up her discarded shoes and bag and set the mail on the coffee table.

She didn't glance at Wade, although all of her senses were aware that he had followed her after closing the door.

A glance at her watch showed that she was running out of time. "Your discussion is going to have to wait." Maggie wasn't sorry.

She needed a few minutes alone to collect her wits before engaging in any conversation with Wade. "I have to change my clothes. It won't take long. If you want something to drink while you're waiting there's beer, Coke, and iced tea in the refrigerator and instant coffee in the cupboard. Help yourself."

All of that was issued over her shoulder as she walked across the living room toward her bedroom. Wade's refusal drifted after her.

"No, thanks, I don't care for anything."

"Suit yourself." She wasn't going to force any refreshment on him . . . or serve him.

She ducked into the hallway, sparing a moment of gratitude that the living room was in order and not strewn with Mike's things, or hers. Tossing her shoes and bag on the bed, she walked to the closet and began rummaging through the hangers for a pair of slacks.

Wade's statement kept running through her mind. He wanted to speak to her about something that was in Mike's interest, yet it had nothing to do with custody.

What could it be? School? Perhaps a private one? Not a boarding school—she would never agree to that. If it didn't have to do with his education, what did that leave?

Maggie was at a loss to come up with an alternative idea.

CHAPTER FOUR

A SOUND IN THE HALLWAY caused her to turn around and her pulse rocketed in alarm at the sight of Wade lounging in the doorway, dark and innately powerful like a predatory beast.

She pivoted back to the closet, grabbing the first slack hanger her fingers touched.

Anger had always been her best defense against his subtle domination.

"I told you I wouldn't be long."

"Don't forget I was married to you." He straightened from the door jamb and wandered into the room. "I know how *long* it can take you to dress. Long becomes a relative term. When you say you won't be long, I always wonder, compared to what?"

His blandness bordered on indifference, yet his criticism irked Maggie. "I never claimed to be as speedy or punctual as you. I doubt if anyone can meet your standards."

She glanced at the blue plaid slacks in her hand and began searching through the closet for a coordinating blouse.

"What is this?"

At his question, Maggie looked over her shoulder. He was pulling out the old robe she had stuffed in the wastebasket. There was a hint of mockery in the ebony depths of his eyes.

"You know very well what that is . . . and why it's there!"

She yanked a pale blue blouse from its hanger. The color intensified the green of her eyes, glittering with irritation.

With her change of clothes in hand, Maggie stalked angrily to the bed.

"I promised Mike I would apologize to you for that outburst yesterday, but I don't think I can ever forgive you for showing up unannounced like that. If you knew how much trouble I went to trying to be sure the house was clean, going to the beauty parlor, and buying a new outfit, and you find me looking like something out of a comic strip. It wasn't fair!"

"So in a burst of temper you threw Old Faithful away." Wade gave the quilted robe a considering study. "It has seen some better days."

For a moment Maggie was silenced by the fact that Wade had recognized her favorite robe, even to the point of recalling the name she had given it. She mentally shook away the feeling of surprised pleasure. So he had a good memory. What did it matter?

"Yes, I threw it away."

Her admission was callously indifferent to the memories attached to the garment. "I have a beautiful new robe in the closet. If I'd been wearing that, at least I wouldn't have looked quite so awful."

"I've seen you looking worse." He let the robe fall back into the wastebasket.

"That isn't any consolation!" Maggie snapped.

"Remember the Sunday we went looking at boats and you fell off the dock into the water?" Wade recalled with a husky laugh. "I think you were wearing a new dress."

"I didn't fall!"

Maggie slipped out of the ivory top and tossed it angrily on the bed. With jerky movements she began unbuttoning her blouse.

"My heel hooked in one of the boards and I lost my balance. I don't recall getting any assistance from you. You just stood there laughing!"

"What could I do? I was holding Mike. Good thing, too, or you'd have drowned him." He was still chuckling, maliciously, Maggie thought. "God, you were a sight! Water dripping from everywhere, your hair looking like a red floor mop."

"I didn't think it was funny then! And I don't think it's funny now!"

Impatiently she tugged at the buttons on the cuffs of her sleeves, finally freeing them and shrugging out of the blouse.

It joined the crumpled heap of her top.

"Your sense of humor was missing when you waded ashore. As I recall, you did a slow boil all the way home. We had one whale of an argument when we did get back."

"And you slammed out of the house and didn't come back until after midnight," Maggie reminded him.

"Yes." The faint smile left his mouth. "Our fights always ended one of two ways—either me slamming out of the house, or right here in this bedroom."

"Most of the time you were slamming out of the house."

The waistband of her skirt fastened behind. She managed the button, but in her agitation she caught the zipper in the material of her skirt, then in the silk of her slip.

"Damn!" she whispered in an angry breath.

"No, most of the time the arguments ended in the bedroom," Wade corrected her statement. He saw the difficulty she was having with the zipper. "I'll fix it for you. The way you're going at it, you're going to break the zipper."

Before Maggie could object or agree, he was pushing her hands out of the way.

The touch of his fingers against her spine brought instant acquiescence as a whole series of disturbing sensations splintered through her.

The warmth of his breath trailed lightly over the bareness of her shoulders, his head bent to his task. The musky fragrance of his cologne wafted in the air, elusive and heady.

From the corner of her eye Maggie could see the glistening blackness of his hair and experienced a desire to slide her fingers into its thickness.

His physical attraction was compelling. She was on dangerous ground.

She wished she had objected to his presence in her bedroom, or steered the conversation away from how their arguments had often ended. It aroused intimate memories it was better to forget.

There was a slight tug and her skirt zipper slid freely. In proportion to its downward slide, her pulse went up. There was a crazy weakness in her knees, muscles tightening in the pit of her stomach.

"There you are, with no damage." His hand rested

lightly on her hip, momentarily holding the skirt up. Maggie couldn't move, couldn't breathe. "I had forgotten how little there is to you."

In a thoughtfully quiet voice, Wade referred to the slightness of her build and how easily his hands could span her waist.

Maggie searched for a quick retort, saying the first thing that came to mind in order to deny that his touch was disturbing her.

"There was always enough of me to satisfy you," she insisted with a husky tremor, and immediately wanted to bite her tongue.

"Yes."

His hand slid to her waist to turn her around, releasing the skirt and letting it fall around her ankles. "There was always more than enough of you to satisfy me, wasn't there?"

Both hands rested on her waist, sliding up to her rib cage. The silk of her slip acted like a second skin, the imprint of his hand burning through.

The smoldering light in his eyes stole the breath from her lungs.

"And you received an ample share of satisfaction, too," he added.

That look awakened all the sleeping desires that had lain dormant.

As his mouth descended toward hers, Maggie trembled.

Would his kiss be the same? Could it still spark the blazing flame of her passion?

Curiosity and familiarity overpowered any thought of protest. She was caught up in the sweeping tide of the past when kissing Wade had been as natural as arguing with him.

Her lips yielded to the possessive pressure of his kiss. That same fiery glow spread through her, hot and brilliant.

His grip on her tightened, threatening to crack her ribs, as if he, too, experienced the same glorious reaction. Her arms glided slowly around his neck, her fingers seeking the sensuous thickness of his hair.

The sweetly pagan song in her ears was the wild drumming of her heart while the heat coursing through her veins turned her bones to liquid. Her slender curves fitted themselves to the hard contours of his length, firing her senses with ecstasy.

There had never been any lack of skill in Wade's lovemaking before, but it was better now. More wonderful. More destroying.

Because now that Maggie had been without that special thrill for these past years, she realized the worth of what she had lost. Having lost it, it was even more beautiful to find it again.

His kisses were like rare wine, and they went to her head. She was spinning away into a rose-colored dreamworld where only the crush of his hands and mouth held any reality.

Then the kiss was ending, before her hunger was satisfied.

Wade was lifting his head, staring deeply into her slowly opening eyes, which were as yet unwilling to return to the present.

Gradually her vision focused on the frown darkening his face.

"Old habits die hard, don't they?" he mused with a trace of cynicism.

His hands were still supporting her passion-limp body. A flurry of new questions raced through her dazed brain. The fresh memory of his kiss wiped away others that dealt with the bitterness and anger of their divorce. She wondered if she had deliberately blocked out the good times of their marriage, needing to remember the bad to keep from missing Wade.

He had said that he wanted to speak to her about something in Mike's interest. An entirely new possibility presented itself to her. After that shattering kiss, could it be that he was going to propose a reconciliation between them?

Yesterday Maggie would have found the suggestion appalling and rejected it out of hand.

Now . . . . Now, the idea filled her with hope, cloud-touching hope.

Suddenly she had to know.

"Why, Wade?" There was an aching tightness in her throat. "Why are you here? Why did you want to see me?"

He let go of her and pulled her arms from around his neck. A muscle twitched along his jaw, constricting in sudden tension.

Not until all physical contact between them had been broken did he answer her question.

"I came to tell you that I'm getting married again." Maggie went white with shock, but Wade was already walking toward the door and didn't see her reaction. "I think I'll take you up on that offer of a drink while you finish changing."

He disappeared into the hallway.

She thought she was going to be violently sick. That announcement had never occurred to her. To be truthful, she had never considered the possibility that Wade would remarry.

Although why she hadn't, she didn't know. That supremely male aura of his had always drawn women. Besides that, he was eligible and successful. Those two reasons alone were sufficient cause for many women to want him.

Hysterical laughter welled in her throat, and she jammed a fist into her mouth to choke it back. It was all so pathetically funny! She had thought he might want to come back to her.

How arrogantly stupid! Physical desire hadn't been able to keep their marriage afloat before.

What had ever made her think it would bring them back together?

Thank God that pride had kept her silent, demanding his reasons before stating her desire. Imagine the humiliation if she had told him what she felt.

Maggie moaned and buried her face in her hands. She wanted to rush over and shut the door, close out the fact of Wade's announcement until she had the strength to cope with it, to face and accept it. But it couldn't be done.

There wasn't time to pull her scattered feelings together. He was waiting for her.

"Old habits die hard," Wade had said after he had kissed her. Maggie knew that was how she had to regard it.

A kiss between two ex-lovers who had found themselves in familiar positions on familiar grounds. The kiss had been a natural progression of events, but without the meaning it had held in the past—at least, not on Wade's part.

In a numbed state, Maggie finished changing her clothes.

She added a brush of shadow and mascara to her eyes and a coating of tinted gloss to her lips, a splash of color in her otherwise pale face.

She ran a quick comb through her flame red hair. Drawing deeply on her reserve strength, she walked out of the bedroom to rejoin Wade.

He wasn't in the living room. She continued through the dining room into the kitchen.

He was standing at the counter, turning when she entered, a glass in his hand.

"I decided I needed something stronger than beer." He lifted the glass, a lone ice cube clinking against the side, amber liquid covering the bottom.

On the counter behind him, Maggie saw the opened bottle of Scotch.

Wade caught her glance. "You still keep it in the same place—behind the flour canister."

"Yes." Was that raspy sound her voice?

"Do you want me to pour you a drink?"

"No."

God, no! Maggie thought vehemently.

As wretched as she felt, one drink wouldn't be enough. She'd want to drown herself in the oblivion of alcohol and it would probably take more than one bottle to dull the pain.

"I'd rather have coffee, thanks."

Walking to the sink, she partially filled a saucepan with hot water and put it on the stove.

Then she reached into the cupboard and took out the jar of instant coffee.

Normally she disliked it, but she kept it on hand for mornings that she overslept and didn't have time to make coffee in her percolator. Now, she realized she was using it for a different kind of emergency as she spooned the brown crystals into a cup along with three teaspoons of sugar.

"You never used to sweeten your coffee," Wade observed.

His memory was much too good.

"It's the only way I can stand drinking instant coffee," Maggie lied.

In actual fact, she had heard that black, sweetened coffee was good for shock, and at the moment she felt numbed to the bone.

CHAPTER FIVE

SHE FELT THE PENETRATION of his gaze between her shoulder blades, but she hadn't yet the composure to face him squarely.

There was an indefinable tension in the air, even a second's silence hanging heavy. Bubbles formed quickly in the pan of water on the stove. Maggie removed it from the burner before it came to a boil and poured the steaming water into her cup.

As she stirred the coffee, she took a deep breath and exhaled the words, "So you're going to get married. It looks as if congratulations are in order, then."

Although she turned to lean her hips against the counter, she again avoided directly meeting his steady gaze, holding the cup in one hand and continuing to stir the coffee with the other.

"We agreed five . . . six years ago to seek our happiness elsewhere."

"It was obviously the right decision, wasn't it?" Maggie countered, much too brightly. "I mean, you've found someone else. She must make you happy or you wouldn't be planning to marry her."

"That's right."

There was a certain grimness in his answer as he lifted his glass to his mouth.

But the admission brought a sharp, stabbing pain in the region of Maggie's heart. It glittered briefly in her jewel green eyes before she lowered her lashes to conceal the reaction.

"Who's the lucky girl?"

Maggie sipped at the coffee and nearly scalded her tongue.

"Her name is Belinda Hale."

"Belinda," Maggie repeated, and lied, "that's a pretty name. Is she from Alaska?"

"No, from Seattle, but I met her while she was visiting some friends in Anchorage."

"It sounds like a whirlwind courtship." As theirs had been. She couldn't help questioning dryly, "Is that wise?"

"Don't worry—" there was a wry twist to his mouth as he swirled the liquor in his glass "—I don't intend to make the same mistake twice. I've known Belinda for over a year now."

"Oh. Well, I'm glad." The coffee had cooled sufficiently for her to drink, but Maggie nearly gagged on the sweetness. "I understand that you're doing quite well. Mike mentioned something about you getting a promotion."

"Yes, I'm a vice-president in the firm now. I have total charge of the Alaskan operation, pipeline, terminals, new drillings, everything."

He explained with no attempt to boast or impress Maggie with his importance.

It had always seemed foredestined to Maggie that such a thing would happen.

Wade had always enjoyed challenges and responsibilities.

Since he was aggressive and ambitious, as well, it was a natural outcome of his efforts.

"Your fiancée must be very proud of you. Of course, being the wife of an executive isn't an easy job. I hope your Belinda is up to the task." She couldn't care less. In fact, part of her hoped his new wife would prove inadequate.

The jealous part of her.

"Belinda is well versed in the role of an executive's wife. Her father is chairman of the board."

Her eyes widened at the announcement, the bitterness of sarcasm coating her tongue. "How convenient. Did your vice-presidency come before or after you put the diamond on her finger?"

Black anger burned in his gaze. "The promotion came a year ago. It was at a cocktail party celebrating my new office that I met Belinda for the first time. I'm not attempting to marry into power. I stand or fall on my own ability."

"Sorry, that was a cheap shot," admitted Maggie. She took another sip of the heavily sweetened coffee and began to feel its bracing effect.

"I do wish you every happiness, Wade. You know that." In a more rational moment, she would mean it very sincerely, even if the words did stick in her throat now.

"I didn't come here this afternoon to obtain your blessing." His voice was mockingly dry. "If all I wanted to do was inform you of my coming marriage, I could have accomplished that with a long-distance phone call from Alaska."

Maggie stiffened, resenting his implied criticism.

"Why are you here?" Then she remembered. "You said you wanted to speak to me about Mike."

"Yes. I haven't told him yet that I'm getting married again."

Her interrupting laugh was short and bitterly incredulous.

"I hope you aren't planning to ask me to tell him."

"No. I'm telling you first because I want your support. I know it won't be easy for Mike to accept the fact that I'm marrying another woman.

"From some of the things he's said, I know he isn't going to welcome having a stepmother," Wade corrected her in a clipped, precise tone.

"And how am I supposed to change that?" she demanded.

Didn't he realize it was going to be difficult for *her* to adjust to the fact that he was getting married to someone else?

"By remaining calm. And, for once, not reacting emotionally."

"You've never been able to accept the fact that I'm an emotional person!" Maggie accused.

"I've accepted it. I've just chosen not to live in your tempestuous teapot."

Maggie turned away. That remark had hit below the belt.

She took a large swallow of coffee. "That was unnecessary, Wade," she said tightly.

"Yes," he sighed heavily, "it was. Look, Maggie, we've managed to have a fairly civil relationship since our divorce, and I don't want my marriage to change that. Maybe I'm asking too much, but I'd like you to extend the same distantly friendly terms to Belinda. For Mike's sake, I think it would be best.''

''Oh, yes, the four of us can be just one great big happy family.''

She mocked his ludicrous suggestion.

''Don't exaggerate,'' Wade snapped. ''I'm not suggesting anything of the kind.''

Maggie pivoted around to challenge him. ''What are you suggesting?''

''That you provide some moral and physical support for my marriage,'' he explained with considerable exasperation.

''What do you want me to do? Walk down the aisle with you and give you away?'' she quipped, hiding behind a black wit to conceal the pain of this conversation.

''Don't be flippant.''

''Well, I'm sorry.''

She wasn't. ''But I don't know what you expect me to do. I have no intention of interfering with your marriage in any way. As for Mike, I'll encourage him to welcome your bride into the family. I don't see how I can do more than that. And I doubt if your Belinda would like it if I interfered more than that in your personal life.''

Wade shook his head and downed the rest of his drink. ''One thing is certain—'' he set the glass down hard on the counter, his control stretching thin ''—Belinda is a hell of a lot more open-minded than you are.''

''I suppose you've discussed me with her.'' That thought didn't set well. ''As well as all my little shortcomings.''

''Naturally I discussed with her my first marriage and

our incompatibility, but I didn't go into detail. Belinda is an intelligent and sensible young woman.''

"And I don't possess either of those qualities." Maggie stated what she felt he had implied.

The line of his jaw hardened. "I didn't say that.''

"No, you didn't have to.''

"Once you meet Belinda, I know you'd like her if you would let yourself—'' there was undisguised irritation in his voice and the glittering black of his eyes ''—and not become jealous.''

"Jealous! I would never be jealous of your new bride!'' The denial leaped angrily from her throat. "Don't forget I divorced you because I didn't want you anymore.''

It was lies, all lies. Maggie knew she still wanted him, and probably had ever since their divorce. Only she hadn't permitted herself to admit it. Subconsciously she had compared every man she met with Wade, and they had all been lacking.

Moreover, if his darling Belinda were in the room at this minute, Maggie would be physically or verbally claw ing at the woman like a jealous cat.

It angered her that Wade had been so accurate in guessing that.

"Don't pretend you won't be jealous. It's a normal reaction for anyone whose former mate remarries.'' Wade swept aside her denial with swift, slicing strokes, the precise cutting thrusts of a rapier striking coldly and ruthlessly. "It's a natural emotion to feel under the circumstances.''

"Don't be so damned logical!'' Maggie turned and set her cup so violently on the kitchen counter that it overturned.

In agitation she grabbed for the dishcloth and wiped up the spill.

As she started to throw it angrily into the sink, Wade's hand closed around her upper arm to check the display of temper. His grip was firm, yet controlled to imply gentle rebuke.

"One of us has to be," he said. "I was hoping both of us could be logical about this."

Maggie jerked away from his hold, rejecting his impersonal touch.

"How dare you suggest that I haven't been?"

Her eyes were blazing with green fires, the toss of her head making her hair ripple like liquid flame around her shoulders.

"I'm more than aware that you're free and can remarry or not, as it suits you. I've even offered you my congratulations and wished you every happiness with your soon-to-be bride.

"As for Mike, I've even agreed to help him become adjusted to the fact that he'll not only have a mother but a stepmother, as well. What more do you expect from me? Should I throw an engagement party for you?"

There was a flashing glimpse of the thinning line of his mouth before he was turning his back to her, his hands on his hips.

Maggie sensed rather than saw the control he was exercising over his own temper.

He shook his head and emitted a sardonic silent laugh. "I'd forgotten how easily you can rile me. When we weren't making love, we were fighting, weren't we? Did we ever share a peaceful moment together?"

The embittered question deflated Maggie's anger. The stiffness of defiance and challenge left her shoulders and spine, and she felt the sagging weight of defeat. Tears stung her eyes, acid and burning.

"Of course we did . . . in the beginning." But she didn't want to talk about that.

At the moment, the memories of that time were too poignant and too vivid. "When are you planning to marry? You haven't said."

"Soon. Within the month."

Her mouth dropped open.

She had expected his response to be autumn or Christmas, not a date that could be measured in days instead of weeks or months.

The pain of loss splintered through her, followed by a thankfulness that he hadn't seen her reaction to the announcement.

"That isn't much time," she recovered to say. "You're practically presenting Mike with an accomplished fact." But it wasn't Mike she was thinking about, it was herself. "You should have told him sooner, let him know there was someone you were seriously interested in."

"How?" Wade glanced over his shoulder, his mouth twisting in a cynical line. "In a letter? Over the telephone? No, that's too impersonal for something that's so important in his life. I wanted us to be face to face when I told him.

"And I wanted him to meet Belinda, get to know her before the wedding. I couldn't do that from Alaska."

"You shouldn't have waited so long," Maggie persisted in the thought.

"Unfortunately I couldn't get away before now. I considered having Mike visit me, but I knew he would want you around once he learned I was engaged. I did the best I could to arrange to spend this time with him before the wedding. As it is, our honeymoon is going to have to be postponed. But Belinda is very understanding about that.''

''She sounds like a paragon of virtue,'' Maggie muttered sarcastically. She simply couldn't help disliking his bride-to-be.

Wade shot her a piercing look before glancing at the heavy gold watch on his wrist. ''Speaking of time, Mike's ball game started ten minutes ago. My car is outside. Do you want to ride with me? There's no point in taking two cars.''

''No, thanks, I prefer to drive my own. Besides, it will save you having to make the trip back here after the game,'' she refused his offer briskly.

Common sense told her that it was better if she didn't spend too much time alone in his company. The time would be too bittersweet.

CHAPTER SIX

A SILVER GRAY MERCEDES was parked in the driveway behind her small car, the luxury model a sharp contrast to Maggie's economy one. She eyed the Mercedes somewhat resentfully.

It seemed to emphasize the chasm that gaped between them. They were poles apart, as they always had been.

"Your company is generous to it executives, furnishing them with a car like that," she remarked dryly as she walked ahead of Wade to the driveway.

"It isn't a company car. It belongs to Belinda," Wade corrected. "Since I was without transportation, she offered me the use of hers."

"What's she driving, then? Her father's Rolls-Royce?"

Maggie sounded catty and she knew it.

It wasn't that she envied the obvious wealth of Belinda's family.

On the contrary, she envied the woman because she would soon have Wade, something all the money in the world couldn't buy.

"She's probably driving her mother's Rolls." His mouth quirked briefly in a mocking smile that didn't make Maggie proud of her remark.

She tried to change the subject. "At which hotel are you staying? In case there's an emergency and I need to reach you," she tacked on so he wouldn't think she was asking for a personal reason.

"I'm staying with the Hales in their home, not a hotel," Wade corrected her with a glint of amusement in his dark eyes.

"Oh."

How foolish of her to have fallen into that! Where else would a prospective son-in-law stay but in the home of his fiancée's parents? Maggie tried not to think how much time that gave him to spend in Belinda's company.

Their paths diverged as they walked to their respective cars.

Maggie's was closest, so she reached hers first and had to wait until Wade had reversed out of the driveway into the street. Jealousy was a demeaning emotion, she realized as she followed the silver Mercedes to the ball park.

Mike's team was at bat when they arrived. Wade waited to walk with Maggie to the bleachers, occupied by only a scattering of other parents. The rest of the boys on the bench with Mike were shouting encouragement to their teammate at bat.

Mike watched him but was silent, a faintly disappointed expression on his face. His gaze strayed to the bleachers.

When he saw Maggie, and a second later Wade, he immediately broke into a wide smile and waved. Maggie returned the salute as she sat down on the second row of the bleacher seats.

Excitedly Mike poked his teammates and pointed to his parents in the stands.

With all the emptiness in the bleachers, Maggie wished Wade had sat somewhere else other than beside her. It was natural that he would, though.

After all, they were both there to see Mike play. He was their son. Not even Wade's approaching marriage changed that.

At the end of the inning Mike dashed to the protective mesh fence near where Maggie and Wade sat. The rest of his teammates were taking the field.

"Hi!" His shining dark eyes gazed at the two people he loved most in the world. "You're late."

"My fault," Wade took the blame.

"I had something to discuss with your mother and we lost track of time."

"That's all right."

Mike shrugged away the explanation as unnecessary now that they were here. Glancing over his shoulder at the ball field, he added a hurried, "I gotta go. I'm playing first base." He raced to join his teammates and take his position.

"You do it, too," Maggie murmured. She caught the lift of a black eyebrow in question and explained, "Mike gets upset when I say your father and keeps insisting you have a name. You just said 'your mother.'"

Wade paused.

"It's easier."

"Yes, I know," she responded quietly.

Their gazes locked for a long span of seconds, each knowing why they wanted to forget the first-name intimacy in referring to the other. It kept the memory of their once shared love at bay. Just for that moment, they remembered it together.

Maggie felt the tugging of her heartstrings. Her heart hadn't forgotten that song of savage ecstasy, not a single note of it. Had Wade?

He turned to watch the game before Maggie could find the answer in his dark eyes.

She chided herself for being so foolish. What did it matter if he did remember? He had found another woman whose love played a sweeter melody, and he was marrying her.

It was best if Maggie's heart forgot the love song.

The ball game was close, but in the end Mike's team lost.

In contrast to the marked jubilation of the winning team, there was noticeable silence among Mike's teammates.

The corners of Mike's mouth were drooping and his shoulders were slumped by the defeat as Maggie and Wade walked around the wire fence to the team bench.

"It was a good game," Maggie offered in consolation.

"We could have won," Mike grumbled, "if I hadn't struck out every time I was at bat."

Tom Darby approached as the last, defeated words were spoken. He smiled briefly at Maggie before clamping a hand on Mike's shoulder.

The coach was as handsome as Maggie remembered, but he stood in Wade's shadow—as every man would, she suspected.

"You'll have to work harder at batting practice, Mike, so you can change that," he said. "But you did a very good job at first base. If it hadn't been for you there, the other team might have scored higher."

The words of praise bolstered Mike's spirits and he managed a smile. "At least they didn't clobber us, did they, coach?"

"They sure didn't," Tom agreed, smiling down at the baseball-capped boy.

He glanced at Maggie. "Mike played a good game. All the boys did." His gaze strayed to Wade, swift and assessing in its sweep of him, as if measuring the strength of his competition.

Mike caught the look, as Maggie had, and quickly supplied the information.

"This is my dad," he beclared with a considerable amount of pride.

In the blink of an eye, Tom's startled gaze darted from Maggie's face to the ringless fingers of her left hand. Then his surprise was hidden by a mask of professionalism as he extended a hand to Wade.

"How do you do, Mr. Rafferty. I'm Tom Darby," he introduced himself.

Maggie stole a sideways glance at Wade as the two men shook hands.

She saw the aloofness in Wade's expression, his dark eyes so cool and withdrawn. Yet behind that chilling veil of indifference they were just as sharp and assessing as Tom's had been.

"It's a rare treat for Mike to have his father attending one of his games," Maggie heard herself saying. "You see, his father works in Alaska and is only here on a short vacation."

She realized she was talking about Wade as if he weren't standing there beside her, but she couldn't seem to stop herself.

Her explanation brought a cloud of confusion to Tom's hazel eyes. Maggie cleared that up with an abrupt, "We're divorced."

There was a moment of awkward silence in which Maggie silently cursed her tactless announcement. Why had she done it so bluntly?

To prove something to Wade? Was it her pride trying to show how eager she was to disassociate herself from him so Wade wouldn't know how his coming marriage hurt?

"Don't mind her," Wade inserted dryly. "She's always said exactly what was on her mind. One of the reasons I married her was because she was so refreshingly honest. After a few years it became one of her irritating traits."

The way he put it sounded like a joke and Tom laughed, but Maggie knew there was more than a measure of truth in it.

She felt the stinging accuracy of his arrow, but forced a smile onto her face as if Wade had said something witty.

"If you have no objections," Tom began, "I thought I'd treat the boys to some ice cream before they go home. Parents are more than welcome to come along."

"Will you?" Mike asked eagerly, wanting to be with his father yet wanting to be with his teammates, and hoping Wade would say yes so the two pleasures could be combined.

"Of course," Wade agreed, a slow smile spreading across his darkly tanned face.

It only took a second for Maggie to consider her answer.

"Not me," she refused.

She didn't want to spend any more time with Wade, certainly not with the complication of Tom Darby around.

She wanted time to be alone and think, to come to grips with the fact that Wade was getting married. "I have some housework to do." She turned to Wade. "You will bring Mike home afterward, won't you?" At his nod, she glanced at Mike. "Have a good time."

"I will."

He was sorry, but not disappointed that she wasn't coming. Why should he be when he saw her virtually every day and his father so seldom?

"I'll see you, Maggie."

Tom's goodbye sounded like a promise, now that he was assured she was free.

"Yes. Goodbye, Tom."

It was only when she was in her car on the way back to the house that Maggie wondered whether Wade had noticed how easily she had used Tom's name.

She supposed he had. Nothing escaped Wade's notice for long. What had he thought? Especially in view of the fact that Tom hadn't been aware she was divorced until now.

Sighing, Maggie shook away such questions. Wade couldn't care less.

His only interest in her was as the mother of his child. Any interest in her private life stopped there. He was getting married; that was still a difficult thing to accept.

There was housework to do.

Also, Maggie hadn't eaten. A cold sandwich and a helping of cottage cheese were singularly unappetizing, but she forced herself to eat them. She washed the dishes and put them away—not that there were many to do, a couple of juice glasses and cereal bowl from this morning, a plate from tonight, and the cup from her instant coffee and Wade's glass.

With the dishes done, she had eliminated all trace of Wade from the kitchen, but she couldn't banish his specter from the rest of the house, especially the bedroom. She found herself glancing out the windows for a glimpse of the silver Mercedes bringing Mike home. The telephone rang and she answered it impatiently.

"Is Wade there?" It was a feminine voice on the other end of the line.

A chilling portent shivered through her. "No, he isn't. Who's calling, please?" She knew what the answer would be.

"This is Belinda Hale. Are you . . . Maggie?" the polite but falsely friendly voice inquired.

"Yes, I am."

She was stiff, on guard, disliking intensely the cultured, musically pitched voice in her ear.

"Has Wade . . . mentioned anything to you about me?"

Again there was an infinitesimal pause, calculated to be secretive.

"About your engagement? Yes, he has, Miss Hale. Congratulations." Her teeth were grinding against each other, but Maggie was determined not to sound like a bitchy ex-wife.

She would be pleasant and nice, even if it killed her.

"Thank you," Belinda answered, so very graciously that it grated. "Wade had said he was going to speak to you about us before he told Michael. But I wasn't certain if he'd had an opportunity.

"He also mentioned some baseball game or other that Michael was playing in, so I didn't know whether he'd talked to you privately yet."

"Yes, we spoke before the game started." Maggie's fingers tightened around the receiver.

If it had been the woman's throat, she would have been strangled by now.

As it was, there was little Maggie could do to silence her, short of hanging up.

Wade had said his future wife was blond. Hearing her voice, Maggie could almost picture her. Blond, probably with blue eyes, always wearing the right clothes with just the right amount of makeup, always poised and prepared for any contingency.

Wade would never find his Belinda with rollers in her hair, wearing an old bathrobe, on her hands and knees.

He had said Belinda was the opposite of Maggie, and listening to the cool, unflustered voice, Maggie believed it.

"Oh. Is the game over?" Belinda Hale asked smoothly, with the proper note of innocent surprise.

"Yes." Maggie's answer was curt.

"I imagine Wade is on his way home, then, and it was needless for me to call."

Maggie wondered if the other woman knew how stinging it was to hear Belinda's home referred to as Wade's. She decided it had been deliberate.

"As a matter of fact, I don't believe he is," she said with a trace of smugness.

"Oh?"

"Mike's coach is treating the team to some ice cream, and Wade went along. He promised to bring Mike home afterward. Shall I have him call you when he does?"

"Would you, please, if it isn't too much trouble?" So polite, so courteous, so pseudowarm. "One of my very dearest friends stopped by this evening. I'm hoping that Wade will come back in time to meet her."

"I'm sure he will if he can."

"Yes. Wade can be such a darling at times, and," Belinda added with a throaty laugh, "so infuriatingly stubborn at other times. But, of course, I don't need to tell you that. You were married to him."

Again Maggie felt the prick of a sharp blade, jabbing at her while her assailant smiled benignly. "Were married"—but no longer.

"Yes, I was married to him, but that was a long time ago."

It didn't seem that long. Maybe because it hadn't been very long since he'd held her in his arms and kissed her and all that old magic had come racing back, more potent than before.

"I really am looking forward to meeting you, Maggie. I know that must sound strange, but I do mean it. It's just that I don't see any reason for there to be any enmity between us. Obviously we aren't in competition for anything. Both you and Wade wanted the divorce. For Michael's sake I think it would be very important for us to be friends."

"I'm looking forward to meeting you, too, Belinda." There was a saccharine quality to her tone. For once, Maggie held her usually candid tongue and didn't voice her opinion about becoming friends with Wade's future bride.

A suspicion was beginning to form. Openminded, Wade had described her. Almost ridiculously so, Maggie concluded.

Not for a minute did she believe a hand of friendship was being extended to her.

More than likely the gesture was part of Belinda's act to impress Wade with her unselfishness, her lack of jealousy and possessiveness.

While it cemented her relationship with Wade, it put Maggie on the defensive. If she rejected the attempt at friendliness by Belinda, Wade would view it as spite and ill temper on Maggie's part. The woman was clever, very clever.

"Wade has promised we'll meet sometime soon," Belinda informed her. "And I can hardly wait to meet Michael. Wade has talked about him so much that I almost feel I know him already.

"After Wade and I are married, I naturally want Michael to continue to visit us, just as he always has visited his father in the past."

"Mike has always enjoyed those visits," Maggie returned.

"You and I should get together for a private little chat. I want to learn what Michael's favorite foods are and the things he likes to do, his pet peeves, and so on."

The woman was determined to be the perfect wife *and* stepmother, Maggie decided. It was an admirable thing, unless all this interest was forced.

That was something difficult to judge over the telephone.

"Mike is a very normal boy, easier to please than most."

Maggie wasn't certain if she knew his favorite foods.

They tended to change with his mood and age. She knew his pet peeve—his mother's always being late. And it was one Maggie had no intention of relating to Mike's future stepmother.

"I'm certain he's a darling. Every photograph I've seen of him, Michael has had a striking resemblance to Wade."

"Yes, he has Wade's dark coloring," Maggie agreed. "His personality is very much his own, though."

"After Wade formally introduces us, we shall have to get together and have that little chat. You can sort of forewarn me about the things that irritate Michael . . . and Wade, for that matter.

"I don't mean any offense, but I don't want to make the same mistake you did in your marriage to Wade. Perhaps you can steer me right."

"I doubt very seriously that you would make the 'mistakes' I did," Maggie dryly answered the suggestion.

From the limited information she had been able to glean, Belinda didn't seem the type to let her emotions run away with her tongue, as Maggie was prone to do.

"I hope not." Belinda laughed, and again it was that practiced laugh that sounded in the throat, rich and husky like velvet. "But you probably do know more about Wade's darker side than I do. I'd be grateful for any tidbit you would want to share."

"Of course." Maggie couldn't tolerate any more of the phone conversation. "I'm sure you want to get back to your friend. I'll have Wade call as soon as he brings Mike home."

"Thank you, I do appreciate that. I hope I'll be talking to you again very soon, Maggie."

"Yes—me, too, Belinda," Maggie lied through her teeth, and waited until she heard the disconnecting click before she slammed the receiver onto its cradle out of sheer frustration and jealousy.

There was no solace in the fact that she hadn't lost her temper. All she felt was a growing sense of despair.

The only way to cope with the situation seemed to be to get through it with as much grace as possible, which wasn't one of her fortes, and to take each day after that as it came.

A CAR DOOR SLAMMED outside. Maggie guessed it was Wade bringing Mike back.

Remembering the last time when he had simply dropped Mike off and left, she was tempted not to go to the door and tell him about the telephone call he had received.

She had to, of course. She didn't want to be accused of being too mean to pass on messages from his fiancée.

Wade was just stepping out of the car when Maggie opened the front door. "There was a telephone call for you, Wade."

An absent frown creased his forehead. "Was there a message?"

Maggie hesitated for a fraction of a second, aware of Mike slowly making his way up the sidewalk to the house. "Miss Hale asked you to call her."

"May I use your phone?"

To call your fiancée? No! Maggie wanted to scream,

but she controlled the impulse and nodded. "Of course. Come in."

At that moment Mike ducked under her arm and slipped into the house. Automatically she prompted him, "Change out of your uniform into some everyday clothes."

"I will," was his desultory murmur.

Her nerves grew taut as Wade drew closer, his nearness vibrating them like a tuning fork when he walked past her into the house. She closed the door, fighting the weakness in her knees.

"You may use the extension in the kitchen if you'd like some privacy," she offered, but Wade was already walking toward the beige phone in the living room.

"It isn't necessary." He picked up the receiver and began dialing the number with an economy of movement. Maggie wanted to make herself scarce, but his indifference trapped her into listening to a one-sided conversation.

"This is Wade. I want to speak to Belinda," he said into the mouthpiece.

While he waited, his sharp gaze swerved to Maggie. "Did she say why she called?"

"Something about a friend she wanted you to meet." Her answer was deliberately vague.

His gaze narrowed briefly as if he sensed Maggie's resentment. Then his attention was diverted by a voice on the other end of the phone.

"Hello." He was returning a greeting, his voice intimately quiet.

A pain twisted through Maggie at the sensual softening of his mouth, almost into a smile. "Yes, she did," Wade replied to a question put to him. "I'm here now—" he glanced at his watch "—about twenty minutes, depending on the traffic." With penetrating swiftness his gaze slashed back to Maggie. "You did? I'm glad."

There was a skeptically mocking lift of one eyebrow, and it didn't require much deduction for Maggie to guess they were talking about her. "Yes, I'll be there as soon as I can, darling."

Her fingers curled into her palms at the parting endearment. Waves of jealousy and envy washed through her, nearly swamping her control.

She turned her back to Wade, her stomach a churning ball.

"Belinda said she had a 'nice' conversation with you. The adjective was hers, not mine," Wade commented.

"What did you think I would do? Hang up on her?" Maggie snapped.

"I wouldn't have been surprised if you had," he countered dryly.

She spun around.

Her temper had been held in check too long, and it flared now as fiery as her red hair. "That was one thing I could always count on, wasn't it? Your unwavering support."

"You've never been known for your tact."

"Neither have you. But your darling Belinda is diplomatic enough to make up for it," Maggie declared with decidedly biting emphasis on his fiancée's name. "She sounds too good to be true. You'd better hang on to her."

"A compliment like that, coming from you, always makes me suspect it's an insult."

The remark was totally unfair because it was the closest Maggie had come to sincerity since she had learned of his approaching marriage.

She didn't like Belinda; she never would, but she didn't doubt that the woman was going to attempt to be all things to Wade.

"Did it ever occur to you that you're the only one who brings out the worst in me?" Maggie retorted in self-defense.

A nerve twitched convulsively in his jaw. "*I* bring out the worst in you?"

The ominous black of anger was in his eyes as he took a step closer.

Although intimidated, Maggie held her ground. "Then explain why you're still single. I don't see anybody beating a path to your door. From all that Mike has said, you date men very infrequently. Why? Because they know a shrew when they see one. I was too blind!"

"I have as many dates as I want, when I want them and with whom!

"After wiggling out from underneath your thumb, I value my freedom."

"No commitments, is that it?" He towered above her, male and dominating.

"That's it!"

"Men like Mike's coach must like that. You make it easy for them."

Maggie was trembling with rage.

"You above all people should know I'm not easy!" she hissed.

"No, you're not easy," Wade agreed, his hand shooting out to imprison her wrist and twisting it behind her back.

The sudden physical contact changed the volatile atmosphere to something as elemental as time eternal. Maggie was trapped by that searing desire and couldn't escape its velvet snare. The black coals of his eyes burned over her face, catching that breathless look of expectancy in her expression.

"I may have brought out the worst in you," he growled, "but I also brought out the best."

"Yes."

The admission crumpled some inner defense mechanism and Maggie's head dipped in defeat to rest against the solid wall of his chest. "I never meant to argue with you, Wade. How do we always manage to start shouting at each other?"

His hand released her wrist and hesitated on her back, his touch not quite a caress nor totally impersonal. All she wanted was for Wade to hold her in his arms for a little while.

But in the next second he was withdrawing his hands and walking away.

"I have no idea how any of our arguments have started."

The indifference of his tone said it didn't matter. His gaze was hooded when he glanced at her, the fires banked or out completely. "Belinda is waiting for me—I have to leave."

Her backbone stiffened. "Of course."

Wade started for the door and paused. "I was late bringing Mike because we stopped somewhere to talk. I told him about Belinda."

"What did he say?"

"Nothing. Not a word. He didn't say he was sorry or glad. He didn't ask when I was getting married. Nothing." Wade breathed in deeply. "Absolutely nothing."

"It was a shock."

She, too, had been speechless when Wade had first told her.

She'd had time to recover.

"I hadn't realized what a shock it would be," he murmured.

"I'll talk to him," said Maggie.

"Tell Mike I'll call him tomorrow afternoon. If it's nice, we'll go boating. I've arranged . . . oh, hell, what does that matter?" Long, impatient strides carried him to the door.

Without glancing back, he repeated, "I'll call him tomorrow."

The door slammed shut before Maggie could find her voice to acknowledge his statement. She stared into the emptiness of the room, still filled with the ghost of Wade's presence.

When the powerful engine of the Mercedes growled outside, she slowly turned toward the bedrooms of the house.

CHAPTER SEVEN

MIKE'S BEDROOM DOOR was closed. Maggie hesitated outside, then knocked once.

Silence was her only answer. She knocked again, more loudly the second time. Several seconds later she received a reluctant response.

"Yeah?"

"It's me. May I come in?" She waited, holding her breath, dreading these next few minutes probably as much as Mike was.

"Yeah."

Turning the doorknob, she pushed the door open and walked in.

Mike was lying on his bed, his hands behind his head, staring at the flat white of the ceiling. He was still dressed in his baseball uniform, the cap on his head, dirty tennis shoes on his feet.

He didn't glance at her.

"I thought you were going to change your clothes," Maggie reminded him.

"I forgot." Mike didn't make any move to correct the oversight.

Maggie didn't want to force the subject, not yet. She walked to the foot of the bed. "The uniform can wait, but these shoes have to go." She began untying the laces.

"You already know, don't you?"

His gaze ended its study of the ceiling to dart accusingly at her.

"If you mean do I know that your father is planning to get married—yes, I do." She kept her voice calm with effort. "He told me before the game. That's why we were late."

"Why? Why does he have to get married? Why can't things stay the way they are?" Mike protested.

"You don't want things to stay the way they are."

"Yes, I do!"

"If they did, you'd never be able to improve your hitting," she reasoned. "You'd never grow up. Everything changes, people, places and things. That's part of growing up. So is accepting those changes."

"He doesn't have to get married. You haven't."

"That doesn't mean I might not someday." She pulled off the tennis shoes and set them on the floor at the foot of his bed. "Your father has met someone he loves very much, so it's only natural that he would want to marry her."

"I don't care!"

"You want your father to be happy, don't you?"

"Getting married doesn't mean he's going to be happy. He was married to you and neither of you were happy," Mike reminded her, a low blow in Maggie's book.

"It isn't fair to assume that if your father and I weren't happy, neither will he be happy with his new wife. It isn't all that much of a change."

Maggie diverted the subject. "It only means there'll be a woman living all the time with your father. You might even like her after you meet her."

"Have you met her?" Mike wanted to know, skeptical.

"No."

"Do you think you're going to like her?"

"How do I know? I haven't met her." Maggie avoided the question, knowing that she, too, was already prejudiced against the woman.

"Dad says she's young and pretty. They might have kids of their own," he speculated. He stared again at the ceiling, eyes troubled and increasingly dark. "They'd be living with him all the time."

Maggie was beginning to understand some of Mike's uncertainties.

"Your father would continue to love you, no matter how many children he and his new wife might have." That, too, was a thought that didn't bring joy into her heart.

"Besides, when you go to visit him, you would have a brother or sister, or both, to play with. When they get older, you can teach them how to play baseball and things like that."

"Aw, mom, that's boring!"

"How do you know? It might be fun," she argued.

"I just wish he wasn't getting married."

"He is, so you might as well accept that." *So had I,* Maggie thought.

"I don't have to like it, though." There was a stubborn set to Mike's chin as he unclasped his hands from behind his head and sat up, curling his sock covered feet beneath him.

"No, you don't have to like it," Maggie agreed, "but you should keep an open mind about it. You haven't even met the woman your father wants to marry."

"Stop calling him that!"

Mike began unbuttoning the shirt of his baseball uniform, his head bent to the task.

"All right." Maggie accepted the reproval. "You haven't met the woman *Wade* wants to marry. You could like her. She might be a lot of fun."

If the impression Maggie had gained from the telephone conversation was accurate, with her poise and sophistication Belinda would not easily relate to a ten-year-old's idea of a person who is a lot of fun. There were enough negatives buzzing around in Mike's head without adding more.

"Why couldn't he marry you?" It was more a protest than a question.

Mike tugged his shirttail from the waistband of his pants.

"Because he loves somebody else. Besides, maybe I wouldn't want to marry him."

It was a tantalizing thought, one she didn't dare think about.

"You were fighting again, weren't you?" It was almost an accusation. "I heard you and dad talking, and you sounded angry."

Maggie wasn't certain how to handle that, so she decided to avoid it.

"Which reminds me, your fa—Wade said he would call you tomorrow afternoon. He mentioned something about going boating."

"Boating! Oh, wow! That's great!" Mike declared exuberantly, completely diverted from his previous subject.

Maggie understood his enthusiasm. Most of his friends

went boating almost every weekend. It was a symbol of status in the community not to be a two-car family, but a two-boat family. Mike probably wasn't aware of that, but he did know his friends were always talking about what they did. Now he would have a story of his own to tell the others.

"That's tomorrow." Playfully Maggie pulled the bill of his cap low on his forehead. "Tonight, it's out of that uniform and into the tub."

"Cut it out," he grumbled in protest, but there was a grin on his face as he pushed her hand away.

THE NEXT MORNING Maggie was in the utility room, folding the clean clothes from the drier.

The washing machine was in its spin cycle, and its thumping roar combined with the music from the radio and the whir of the drier drowned out all other sounds.

It wasn't until the washing machine stopped that Maggie heard the phone ringing in the kitchen. She dashed quickly to answer it.

"Rafferty residence," she rushed, half expecting to hear a dial tone to indicate the caller had hung up.

"Maggie? It's Wade."

Her already racing pulse redoubled its tempo. Determinedly she tried to check its thudding rise. "Mike's outside. I'll get him for you."

Before she could put the receiver down, Wade was ordering, "Wait a minute."

"Yes?"

A self-conscious hand touched the flaming silk tumble of hair on top of her head, secured there by a green ribbon.

It was crazy—Wade couldn't see her.

"Did you talk to Mike last night?"

"Yes, I did." She marshaled her scattered thoughts. "He was upset, naturally. It was such a surprise to him. No child likes things to change unless it's instigated by him. It makes him insecure."

"Mike's life isn't changing that drastically because of my marriage."

"But Mike sees that it potentially could," Maggie pointed out. "His main worry seems to be that you might have other children and forget him."

"Maggie, you know . . . " Wade began impatiently.

"I'm not saying it would happen," she interrupted. "I'm saying that it concerns Mike. He isn't an impulsive boy. It's going to take him time to adjust to the idea of a stepmother.

"You've known her for more than a year, Mike hasn't even met her. One or two meetings aren't going to be enough for him, either."

"No, it will take time," Wade agreed in a grimly resigned voice. "How was he after your talk?"

"Eager for today to come so he could go boating with you." Then Maggie realized the time. "You haven't had to change your plans, have you? You said you'd call this afternoon."

"I haven't changed my plans. At least, I'm not canceling the outing," he qualified his statement. "I thought Mike might like to leave sooner, have lunch aboard the boat."

"He'd love it."

"Do you mind?"

"No, I don't mind," Maggie insisted, and wondered

where the silly lump came from in her throat. "You'll want to talk to him. I'll tell him you're on the phone."

"There's no need." Once again Wade stopped her. "Just tell him I'm leaving now and for him to be ready when I arrive."

"I will."

"Maggie? Thanks," he said simply.

She hesitated.

"You'll have to do the same for me someday when I decide to get married." The idea seemed so remote at the moment that it was laughable. Instead, Maggie felt tears pricking her eyes.

"You can count on it," Wade promised.

It was several minutes after he had said goodbye before Maggie had enough composure to walk to the back door to call Mike inside.

She had judged his reaction accurately. He was ecstatic over the change of plans.

When he ran to his room to change shirts and put on a clean pair of tennis shoes, Maggie freshened her makeup and took the green ribbon from her hair.

Then it was back to the utility room and the clothes in the drier.

As she was pairing the socks, Mike poked his head around the door.

"I'm going outside to wait for dad."

"Have a good time." Maggie smiled to conceal her envy for his day.

"You bet!"

"I'll see you tonight." But Mike was already gone and parting words bounced forlornly off the walls of the utility room.

Trying not to dwell too much on what she was going to do with herself all day, Maggie methodically folded the socks and put them with the stack of clothes in the wicker basket.

When it was filled, she picked it up. It was heavy and she hurried in order to bring a quick end to the weight tugging at her arms.

As she rounded the archway into the living room, she was hit broadside by a tall, hard form. The collision wrenched the basket from her straining hands, flipping it upside down and dumping the folded clean clothes onto the floor.

. The force of the collision staggered her, but a pair of large hands immediately steadied her.

Wade's hands—her senses recognized his touch immediately.

On impact, she had issued a startled cry. Her heart was lodged in her throat as she stared at Wade and not a sound could get past it.

A white knit shirt, unbuttoned at the throat, contrasted with the navy pants and Windbreaker he wore. The dark blue color intensified the jet blackness of his attractively unkempt hair, looking as if it were freshly rumpled by a sea breeze. A concerned look was etched in his harshly vital and male features, his dark eyes piercing in their scrutiny.

With an effort Maggie forced her gaze from his compelling face, fighting the breathless waves of excitement that engulfed her.

Her glance fell on the once neatly folded clothes scattered over the floor. They would all have to be folded, separated, and stacked in the basket again. Angry exasp-

eration at the wasted time she'd spent overtook the rest of
her tangled emotions and her hands slid to her hips in an
attitude of temper.

Before she could speak, Wade was saying, "I'm sorry,
I didn't know you were going to come racing around the
corner at that moment."

Racing around the corner! The phrase indicated the
blame was hers.

What had been a mere spark of anger blazed into full
flame.

She turned on him, her green eyes flashing. As her
mouth started to open, his fingers closed it.

There was a wicked twinkle in his dark eyes. "I said I
was sorry," he reminded her. His thumb lightly caressed
the curve of her mouth before he took his hand away and
glanced at his son.

"Come on, Mike. Let's help your mom pick up the
clothes."

That vague caress had turned away her anger. Maggie
was left standing there, impotent, while Mike and Wade
bent to begin picking up the scattered clothes. It was
several seconds before she recovered sufficiently to help
them.

"We were just coming in to tell you we were going,"
Mike explained.

"You'll be home before dark, won't you?" Maggie hadn't asked Wade how long they intended to be
gone.

"We'll be back to the marina before dark." He satisfied her mind on that worry. "Don't wait dinner for Mike,
though. We'll probably have something to eat before I
bring him home."

"Oh."

That meant two meals she would have to eat alone, lunch and dinner.

"Dad, are we going out on the boat alone, just you and me?"

Mike bunched a group of socks together and stuffed them in the basket. Maggie rescued them and tried to sort them into pairs.

"Yes, it will just be the two of us."

"Why can't mom come along?"

CHAPTER EIGHT

"MIKE!"

She was so startled by Mike's unexpected request to include her in their plans that his name was the only word of protest she could think to make.

Color rouged her cheeks for fear Wade might think she had previously hinted to Mike for the invitation. A sideways glance at Wade showed his curious frown.

Mike pursued his request, ignoring her outburst. "She's on vacation and she doesn't have anything to do, especially with me going places with you." He continued without giving Wade a chance to reply, "I know mom likes boats 'cause I've seen the pictures of the boat you two used to have."

"Mike," Maggie interrupted sharply, "your father wants to spend time alone with you. You and I will have time to do things together later."

"Yeah, but—" he was struggling for the words "—we've never done things together like a family. At least, I was too little to remember if we did. And—"

"But we aren't a family," Maggie protested.

"Yes, we are," Wade corrected her in a quiet but firm voice. "You are the mother, I am the father and Mike is the son. A divorce doesn't change that."

"No, but . . . ." She felt panic.

"Can she come along, dad?" Mike interrupted eagerly, his eyes alight with cautious hope.

"Of course she can come along," Wade agreed, and glanced at Maggie.

"Will you go boating with us?"

She was thrown into confusion. He couldn't really mean it, but there wasn't any reluctance in his voice or his expression.

"Oh, but I—" she began.

"Please, mom!" Mike inserted to ward off her refusal.

"Please, Maggie."

Wade lent his voice to Mike's. His expression was serious, not a hint of mockery to be seen.

She might have resisted Mike's plea, but to deny Wade's was impossible.

Her head was bobbing in agreement before she could get the words out.

"Very well, I'll come with you." Not without misgivings.

Her glance went down the crisp blue Levi's she wore and plain knit top. "I'll have to—"

Wade saw the direction her thoughts were taking and interrupted.

"There's nothing wrong with what you're wearing. A pair of tennis shoes and a Windbreaker are the only additions we'll need. Mike and I don't want to wait the time it would take you to change entirely."

This time there was a glint of mockery in his dark eyes.

"It doesn't take me that long," Maggie denied with a defiant tilt of her chin.

"Only forever," Mike exaggerated.

"That isn't true!" There was an indignant gleam in her look.

"The invitation was issued with the proviso to 'come as you are,' " Wade told her. "Mike, go and get her shoes and a Windbreaker."

"Right, dad."

And he put his agreement into action.

Common sense agreed that there was nothing wrong with what she was wearing. Her Levi's and top were neat and clean.

Vanity, however, insisted there were outfits in her wardrobe equally serviceable and much more fashionable. But between Wade and Mike, they had taken the choice out of her hands.

Wade added the last of the clothes to the basket and set it aside. Maggie watched him. He lifted the heavy basket so easily.

All thought of clothes was pushed from her mind, the void to be filled by recognition of his powerfully muscled frame and his innate virility.

She realized how dangerous it was to spend an afternoon or an hour with him.

"I don't think this is a good idea," she murmured aloud.

"What?" He cocked his head at an inquiring angle, a brow lifting slightly, a half smile touching his mouth. "Not changing clothes?" he mocked.

"No, my going with you." In self-defense, Maggie hastened to disguise the truth of her answer. "The idea is for Mike to adjust to your coming marriage. My coming along is just going to confuse the issue."

"I don't agree." He eyed her steadily. "Since Mike

has grown up, he's either been with you alone, or with me alone—never in the company of a couple where he isn't the sole object of attention. Today he's going to see what it's like when there are three people together. For the experiment, it's you instead of Belinda.''

''That's very logical,'' she murmured.

His motives for wanting her along became obvious. It wasn't a desire for her company, or for a last time to be together as a family.

No, Wade was sparing his darling Belinda from any outright rejection by his son. Some of the inner joy that Maggie had hardly dared to let herself feel faded at the discovery.

''What's very logical?''

Mike returned with her tennis shoes and yellow Windbreaker.

For a split second Maggie was at a loss for an answer. ''For your father to invite me along so he won't have to cook.''

''Yeah, that is pretty smart, dad,'' he agreed with a grin.

''I thought so.''

Stepping out of the casual leather loafers, Maggie put on the tennis shoes and tied the laces. The thin, slick jacket she let drape over one shoulder. When she was ready, Mike led the way outside.

If Maggie needed any further reminder that she was only a stand-in for Belinda, the silver Mercedes provided it. She began to wonder if the boat, too, belonged to his future bride.

For once, she didn't have the audacity to ask. Although there was ample room in the front seat for three, she chose to sit alone in the back. It saved making innocuous conversation.

"What do you think of the car, Mike? You never did comment on it yesterday."

Wade turned it onto a busy street, the luxury car accelerating into the flow of traffic.

"It's nice." Mike was obviously unimpressed by the plushness of the interior. "But I like that fourwheel-drive vehicle you have in Alaska a lot better. It can go anywhere!"

Wade chuckled and admitted, "There are times when you can't get around unless you have that kind of vehicle."

Personally Maggie thought Wade was more suited to the type of vehicle Mike had described. Not that he didn't look perfectly at home behind the wheel of this luxury model.

But the plush, elegant car seemed to shield its owner from the realities of life, whereas Wade was the kind of man who met life head-on, taking the knocks and driving forward, going anywhere he pleased.

But such admiration for the character of the man he was was not wise.

Maggie turned her attention to the city sprawling around them. Like the Eternal City of Rome, Seattle had originally been a city of seven hills. Shortly after the turn of the century, Denny Hill was leveled to permit the city to expand.

Water dominated the city, not just because it was a seaport, but because of the two lakes within its limits and a ship canal, as well as its being flanked by Lake Washington on the east and Puget Sound on the west.

Considering that fact, it wasn't surprising that there were more boats per capita than anywhere else in the country.

Maggie was positive they were all crowded into the marina where Wade stopped. Unerring, he led them past the rows of boats, all shapes, sizes, and kinds, to a sleek powerful cruiser.

It was larger and a later model than the one they owned when they were married. Maggie felt she was stepping back in time when she stepped aboard. As he helped her onto the deck, her flesh tingled at the impersonal grip of his hand.

"Where are we going? Just anywhere?"

Mike wanted to know their destination, at the same time not caring.

"We'll decide when we reach open water. How's that?" Wade loosed the mooring ropes. "Or maybe we won't go anywhere special."

"I suppose it's too far to go all the way to the ocean."

"No, it isn't too far, but I think we'll find enough to see and do without that."

The inboard motors roared to life and Wade began maneuvering the cruiser out of the crowded marina waters.

Mike was right at his side observing everything he did. There was a tightening in her throat as Maggie saw how strong the resemblance was between father and son, Mike a young miniature of Wade.

The breeze coming off the water was cool. Maggie started to slip her Windbreaker on, then decided, "I'll go below and start lunch now."

"Good idea," Wade agreed, and combed his fingers

IT'S FUN! IT'S FREE!
AND IT COULD MAKE YOU A
MILLIONAIRE

If you've ever played scratch-off lottery tickets, you should be familiar with how our games work. On each of the first four tickets (numbered 1 to 4 in the upper right) there are Pink Metallic Strips to scratch off.

Using a coin, do just that—carefully scratch the PINK strips to reveal how much each ticket could be worth if it is a winning ticket. Tickets could be worth from $100.00 to $1,000,000.00 in lifetime money.

Note, also, that each of your 4 tickets has a unique sweepstakes Lucky Number . . . and that's 4 chances for a **BIG WIN!**

FREE BOOKS!

At the same time you play your tickets for big prizes, you are invited to play ticket #5 for the chance to get one or more free books from Harlequin®. We give away free books to introduce readers to the benefits of the Harlequin Reader Service®.

Accepting the free book(s) places you under no obligation to buy anything! You may keep your free book(s) and return the accompanying statement marked ''cancel.'' But if we don't hear from you, then every month, we'll deliver 6 of the newest Harlequin Presents® novels right to your door. You'll pay the low subscriber price of just $2.24* each plus 25¢ delivery and applicable sales tax, if any*. That's the complete price, and compared to cover price of $2.89 each in stores—quite a bargain!

Of course, you may play ''THE BIG WIN'' without requesting any free book(s) by scratching tickets #1 through #4 only. But remember, that first shipment of one or more books is FREE!

PLUS A FREE GIFT!

One more thing, when you accept the free book(s) on ticket #5, you are also entitled to play ticket #6, which is GOOD FOR A GREAT GIFT! Like the book(s), this gift is totally free and yours to keep as thanks for giving our Reader Service a try!

So scratch off the PINK STRIPS on all your BIG WIN tickets and send for everything today! You've got nothing to lose and everything to gain!

Here are your BIG WIN Game Tickets, potentially worth from $100.00 to $1,000,000.00 each. Scratch off the PINK METALLIC STRIP on each of your Sweepstakes tickets to see what you could win and mail your entry right away. (SEE OFFICIAL RULES IN BACK OF BOOK FOR DETAILS!)

This could be your lucky day - GOOD LUCK!

FOLD AND DETACH ALONG THIS DOTTED LINE—RETURN ALL GAME TICKETS INTACT.

THE BIG WIN

TICKET 1
Scratch PINK METALLIC STRIP to reveal potential value of this ticket if it is a winning ticket. Return all game tickets intact.

LUCKY NUMBER

7H 166259

THE BIG WIN

TICKET 2
Scratch PINK METALLIC STRIP to reveal potential value of this ticket if it is a winning ticket. Return all game tickets intact.

LUCKY NUMBER

3J 153877

THE BIG WIN

TICKET 3
Scratch PINK METALLIC STRIP to reveal potential value of this ticket if it is a winning ticket. Return all game tickets intact.

LUCKY NUMBER

9W 172463

THE BIG WIN

TICKET 4
Scratch PINK METALLIC STRIP to reveal potential value of this ticket if it is a winning ticket. Return all game tickets intact.

LUCKY NUMBER

1I 150371

FREE BOOKS

TICKET 5
We're giving away brand new books to selected individuals. Scratch PINK METALLIC STRIP for number of free books you will receive

AUTHORIZATION CODE

130107-742

FREE GIFT

TICKET 6
We have an outstanding added gift for you if you are accepting our free books. Scratch PINK METALLIC STRIP to reveal gift

AUTHORIZATION CODE

130107-742

YES! Enter my Lucky Numbers in THE BIG WIN Sweepstakes, and when winners are selected, tell me if I've won any prize. If PINK METALLIC STRIP is scratched off on ticket #5, I will also receive one or more FREE Harlequin Presents® novels along with the FREE GIFT on ticket #6, as explained on the opposite page. 106 CIH AH2D (U-JDA-01/93)

NAME _____

ADDRESS _____ APT. _____

CITY _____ STATE _____ ZIP CODE _____

**Carefully detach card along dotted lines and mail today!
Play all your BIG WIN tickets and get everything you're
entitled to—including FREE BOOKS and a FREE GIFT!**

ALTERNATE MEANS OF ENTRY: Print your name and address on a 3″ × 5″ piece
of plain paper and send to: Harlequin Reader Service®, 3010 Walden Ave.,
P.O. Box 1867, Buffalo, NY 14269-1867. Limit: One entry per envelope.

If game card is missing, write to: Harlequin Reader Service, 3010 Walden Ave., P.O. Box 1867, Buffalo, NY 14269-1867

BUSINESS REPLY MAIL
FIRST CLASS MAIL   PERMIT NO. 717   BUFFALO, NY

POSTAGE WILL BE PAID BY ADDRESSEE

HARLEQUIN READER SERVICE
3010 WALDEN AVE
PO BOX 1867
BUFFALO NY 14240-9952

NO POSTAGE
NECESSARY
IF MAILED
IN THE
UNITED STATES

through his wind-ruffled hair. "We're well stocked with food, so fix whatever you like." As she started down the open hatchway, he called after her, "Maggie? There's some bait shrimp in the refrigerator. I didn't want you to mistake it for the eating kind."

She heard the teasing laughter in his voice and retorted, "Are you sure you wouldn't like a shrimp cocktail?" reminding him of the time the first year they were married when she had unknowingly used bait shrimp for that purpose.

His rich laughter followed her below.

The private joke was beyond Mike, but he was more interested in the use of the shrimp. "Are we going to fish?"

"I thought we might. Fishing is supposed to be good."

"Hey, mom! Why don't you wait to fix lunch until after we catch some fish? Then you can cook what we catch."

"No, thanks. I might starve before then," Maggie called back.

"It doesn't sound as if she thinks too much of us as fishermen, does it?" she heard Wade say

"That's because she's never been fishing with us," Mike replied.

"Didn't you tell her about any of the fish we caught?"

"Oh, sure."

Maggie walked from the galley to the bottom of the steps.

"Mike told me all those fish stories about the times he went with you in Alaska. You only brought back three fish apiece and each of the three fish weighed thirty pounds," she teased.

"It's the truth, mom, honest," Mike insisted.

"The next time we'll have to take a camera along, won't we?" said Wade.

"Then she'll have to believe me, huh?"

"Right."

Maggie went back to fixing lunch, listening to the bantering between father and son. It made her feel warm and secure inside, as if they were really a family. She wished it could always be this way . . . or that it had always been like this.

But it hadn't and it couldn't.

The lunch was simple fare, a mug of hot soup and a cold meat sandwich served on deck. Wade anchored the cruiser in a sheltered cover of Whidbey Island.

A beautiful wilderness beach stretched invitingly along the shore.

"Boy, this soup sure warms up your stomach," Mike declared.

"Tastes good, doesn't it?" Maggie sipped the hot liquid in her mug.

The breeze remained cool and a thickening layer of clouds shut out the warmth of the sun. She eyed the mat gray sky and glanced at Wade. Perceptively he read her thoughts.

"I checked the weather a few minutes ago. There's a front moving in—overcast skies, cooler temperatures, but very little rain is expected with it," he reported.

"That's pretty normal for the area, isn't it?" she smiled.

The Olympic Mountains to the west sheltered the islands in Puget Sound, as well as Seattle, from the brunt of weather fronts moving in from the Pacific.

The mountains divested the clouds of most of their moisture, keeping the rainfall inland to nominal amounts. Few storms of any intensity ever reached the protected sound.

CHAPTER NINE

AFTER LUNCH WAS OVER, Mike was designated cabin boy and ordered to clean the dishes. He grudgingly obeyed, after trying unsuccessfully to enlist help from either of them.

The boat remained anchored in the cove, with Maggie and Wade relaxing on the cushioned seats of the aft deck.

Her yellow Windbreaker was zipped to the throat, her hands stuffed in the front pocket. Thus protected, she leaned back to enjoy the brisk air, tangy with the scent of the sea.

All was quiet except for the lapping water against the boat's hull and the whispering breeze talking to the rustling leaves on the island's wooded interior. And, of course, there was the clatter of dishes in the cabin galley below.

"You've made a good job of raising Mike," Wade remarked quietly.

"I haven't done it alone. You've contributed, too." Maggie met his look, aware of its gentleness.

"The credit belongs to you. He's with you much more than he is with me. But thanks for making me feel I've had a hand in it."

Looking away from her, he took a deep breath and

let it out slowly, like a sigh. "Today you said you would want me to talk to Mike before you got married. Are you planning to marry again?"

"Someday, when I find the right man." The prospect looked dismal. "Like you, I don't want to make another mistake. The next time I want to be very, very sure."

"You don't have anyone in mind, then?" His gaze returned to her, dark and impenetrable.

"Not any one person. There are a few prospects on the horizon, but—" Maggie shrugged "—I'm not going to rush into anything."

"You said something the other day that's been bothering me."

His expression was thoughtful, slightly distant.

"What was that?"

"You said that after you'd wiggled out from under my thumb, you learned to value your freedom. What did you mean by that?"

Before she attempted an answer, Wade went on. "Granted, you said it in a moment of temper. But you rarely say things in the heat of anger that you don't mean.

"When we were married, you were always free to do as you pleased, within reason, of course."

"In theory, I was." At his gathering frown, Maggie tried to explain.

"All day long you gave orders to your employees. When you came home, you continued to give orders. You never seemed to *ask* me to do anything, you were always *telling* me.

"Instead of giving orders to the people who worked under you, you gave them to me—and I was much too independent to stand for that." A wry smile dimpled her cheeks.

"I never intended them to be orders."

"You probably didn't, but that's the way they came out."

"I'm . . . sorry." There was a certain grimness to his mouth.

"Don't be. It's in the past and forgotten." But Maggie guessed he was filing it away for future reference, something he didn't want to repeat in his new marriage to Belinda.

It hurt.

"I'm done!" Mike popped up the steps. "Can we fish now?"

The quiet interlude was over. Wade straightened from his comfortable position with obvious reluctance. "Get the bait out of the refrigerator while I find the rods and reels," he directed.

"Are we going to fish here?"

"Why not? If the fish aren't biting here, we'll move someplace else," Wade reasoned.

As far as Maggie was concerned, she found Mike's presence, his steady stream of chatter and expectant excitement, better than the confiding quietness when she and Wade had been alone.

He kept her mind from thinking intimate thoughts and envisioning hopeless dreams.

The fishing turned out to be not very good in that cove and Wade moved the boat to another. Early afternoon was not the best time of day for fishing, but at the second place they stopped, Mike did catch one that was big enough to keep.

They all threw several back. After they had moved again, Wade caught the next.

A fine mist began to fall, but despite their partial success, the weather didn't interfere with their sport. It dampened their clothes, but not their spirit. The water in the third cove was fairly deep.

A fish nibbled on Maggie's baited hook, then took it. She began reeling it in, feeling it fight and certain this time she had got a big one.

"Got a fish, mom?" Mike glanced over his shoulder from his position on the opposite side of the boat next to Wade.

"A fish or a baby." She had reeled in too many small ones that she thought would be large to brag about this one.

"At the rate your mother is going, you and I are going to be the only ones with food on our plates tonight, Mike," Wade teased.

"Yeah, and she's got to cook it for us."

Maggie kept her silence with an effort, ignoring the way they were ganging up on her. The fish broke surface and she had to swallow back her shout of glee. It looked big enough to keep. Now all she had to do was land it. A few minutes later she had it in her lap—literally, its tail flapping on her jeans while she tried to work the hook out of its mouth.

"What ya got there, mom? A goldfish?" Mike teased.

"No, I have a real fish." She struggled some more but couldn't work the hook free. "He's swallowed the hook."

"It's the only way she could have caught it," Wade laughed. "Watch my rod while I help your mother." He walked over and Maggie surrendered her catch, a shade triumphantly, to him.

"You really hooked him. That's too bad." He crouched on the deck beside her and gently began working the hook in the gaping fish's mouth.

"Why is that too bad?" Maggie demanded to know.

"Because it isn't big enough to keep."

"It is, too!" she declared indignantly. "It's just as big as yours was."

"No, it's a couple of inches smaller," Wade replied.

"You have to throw it back, mom," Mike inserted.

"You just stay out of it," she told him, and turned angrily back to Wade. "You get out your fish and we'll see if mine is smaller."

He smiled. "I don't have to get out my fish. I already know yours is smaller—too small to keep." He freed the hook and tossed the fish over the side.

"My fish!"

Maggie wailed, and dived toward the rail, as if thinking she could catch it before it reached the water.

There was a splash before she even reached the side of the boat. Her hand went out for the railing to stop her progress.

The steady mist had coated the railing with slippery beads of moisture and her hand found nothing to grip on the wet surface of the rail and slid beyond it. The unchecked forward impetus carried her against the low rail, pitching her body over it.

Her startled shriek of fright and alarm was echoed by Mike's "Mom!"

Something grabbed at her foot and in the next second she was tumbling into the water. Immediately instinct took over. Holding her breath, she turned and kicked toward the surface, taking care to avoid the hull of the boat.

She came up spluttering, gasping in air. She was shaking all over, more from cold than the initial fright. The first sound she heard was laughter, Wade's deep, chuckling laughter.

When he saw Maggie was safe and unharmed, Mike joined in.

"Have you found a new way to fish?" Wade mocked.

"You . . . ." In her surge of anger, Maggie forgot to tread water and ended up swallowing a mouthful of the salty stuff.

Coughing and choking, she resurfaced and struck out for the boat ladder. The weight of her saturated clothes pulled at her body.

His hand was there to help her aboard. With the fingers of one hand around the lowest rung, Maggie paused in the water to glare at him and the dancing light in his black eyes.

Ignoring his offer of his assistance, she pulled herself aboard unaided.

Standing on deck, a pool of sea water at her feet, water streaming from her sodden clothes, she looked first at Mike, who was giggling behind his hand. Her hair was plastered over her forehead, cheeks and neck. Water ran into her eyes and she wiped it away to glare again at Wade. A smile was playing with the corners of his mouth, regardless of his attempts to make it go away.

"You think it's all very funny, don't you?" she accused, her teeth chattering with an onsetting chill. "I could have drowned while the two of you were laughing!"

"That's hardly likely, Maggie. You're an excellent swimmer," Wade reminded her in a dry, mocking tone.

"I could have hit my head on the boat or a rock or something!" she sputtered.

"The water is fairly clear," Wade pointed out. "I could see you weren't in trouble. Here." He reached down and picked up a tennis shoe from the deck—Maggie's. "When I grabbed for you, all I got was your shoe. At least it's dry."

Maggie snatched it from his outstretched hand. "What good is one dry tennis shoe—" she waved it in front of his face "—when I have one wet one? Not to mention that my clothes are soaked! A dry tennis shoe just doesn't go with the rest of my outfit!" In a burst of temper, she hurled the lone, dry tennis shoe over the side, where it floated on the quiet surface.

Mike gasped in surprise, then broke out laughing, finding the scene uproariously funny.

It didn't help Maggie's growing sense of frustration one bit.

"You'd better practice your casting, Mike, and see if you can't hook that shoe before it sinks," Wade advised, keeping the amusement in his voice at a minimum. "As for you, Maggie, I think you'd better go below and get out of those wet clothes before you get chilled."

"Chilled! What do you think I am now?" she cried angrily. "My legs are shaking so badly now that I can hardly stand up."

"I'll help you."

Wade took a step toward her.

"No! I don't need any help from you. You take one more step and I'll push you over the side; then you can see what it feels like to be drenched to the skin,'' she threatened, and not falsely.

"And stop giving me orders! I'm an adult. I know I have to get out of these wet clothes, you don't have to remind me of that.''

The latter half of her statement wiped the gleam from his eyes. They were flat black as he stepped to the side, indicating by his action that he would make no move to help her.

Maggie swept by him to the steps with as much dignity as her dripping figure could muster, but her chattering teeth destroyed much of the effect.

Below, she tugged the saturated clothes from her body and piled them in the sink.

Taking a towel from the lavatory, she rubbed her skin dry until it burned. A second towel she wrapped around her straggly wet hair, securing it on top of her head with a tuck in front.

Then came the problem of something dry to wear. She opened a drawer, looking for a blanket. Inside were folded flannel shirts, men's shirts. A red and black plaid was on top.

At this point Maggie wasn't particular. Anything that was warm and dry and permitted movement would do.

The shirt engulfed her, the tails reaching to her knees, the sleeves almost as far. After a few awkward attempts she managed to roll the long sleeves up to her forearms and button the front.

With that accomplished, she began trying to towel her hair dry.

"How are you doing?" Wade called down.

"Fine," she snapped, and muttered to herself, "as a drowned rat."

She was still shivering.

After glancing around, she called, "Is there any cocoa?"

Instead of answering, Wade descended the steps as soundlessly as a cat. "If there isn't cocoa, there's instant coffee. With sugar, it will probably do you more good than cocoa."

"I know there's instant coffee. I would have made a cup if you'd told me there wasn't cocoa."

"Your temper still hasn't cooled off, has it?" he observed dryly, and walked to the cupboards above the galley sink.

"It's the only part of me that hasn't," Maggie muttered.

"I don't see any cocoa."

Wade moved items on the shelf around. "You'll have to settle for coffee."

"I can fix it myself," she insisted when he filled the kettle with water.

"Shut up, Maggie." It was said quietly but no less firmly. "Stop being so damned independent and go sit down." He saw the flashing green fire in her eyes and added, "Yes, it is an order. Because at the moment, you're so angry you'd cut off your nose to spite your face."

"Not mine," she retorted. "But I might cut off *your* nose!"

"I'll get the coffee, then give you the knife." He lit the gas burner and set the kettle over the flame. Shaking his dark head, he murmured, "Only you could get into these kinds of scrapes, Maggie."

Maggie didn't argue any more about making the coffee herself.

Neither did she go sit down as he had ordered. She resumed the brisk rubbing of her hair, deep red gold wavelets rippling over her head.

"I certainly didn't intend to fall overboard," she muttered.

"All because of a silly little fish." The corners of his mouth deepened.

"That you threw away," Maggie reminded him.

"It was too small."

"It was almost big enough to keep," she argued.

"There, you just admitted it yourself." Wade smiled, without triumph.

"Okay, so I admit it."

She tossed the towel aside.

"What are you doing in that shirt?"

The change of subject startled her. Her winged brows drew together in a frown and a short, disbelieving laugh came from her throat.

"I'm wearing it," she retorted.

A raking, impatient glance swept her from head to foot. "I suppose you think you look sexy wearing a man's shirt that comes to your knees, with shoulder seams that practically reach your elbows."

"It never occurred to me how I might look wearing it!" she answered defensively. "It was warm and I could move around freely while I was wearing it. If it reminded me of anything, it was a flannel nightgown. I wasn't even thinking about being sexy. The only male around here that I care about is Michael."

And she denied the thudding pulse racing in her slender neck.

"Believe me, you don't look a bit like my grandmother did in her flannel nightgown." Wade spooned coffee crystals into a mug and gave her a black, smoldering look. A muscle stood out along his jaw. "When a man sees you like that, dressed in a man's shirt without a stitch of clothing under it, looking lost and vulnerable, he wants to hold you in his arms and—" He snapped off the rest of that sentence. "As if you didn't know, you look damned cute!"

"I don't know if that's a compliment or a sin."

Confusion tempered her defensive anger as she turned aside.

His hand gripped her elbow to turn her back.

"The only place you have in my life is as the mother of my child."

The brutally frank statement stung.

"I know that," Maggie retorted, choking, unable to shrug out of his hold.

"Then explain to me why I can't forget that you're my wife?"

His grip shifted to clasp both her shoulders in hard demand.

CHAPTER TEN

HER LIPS PARTED to draw in a fearfully happy breath. As she gazed up at him, a fine mist of tears brought a jewel-like intensity to the green color of her eyes. She heard the groaning sound he made before his finger tightened to dig into her flesh and draw her to him.

The crush of his mouth ignited a sweet fire that raged through her veins.

Curving her arms around his neck, Maggie slid her fingers into his shaggy mane of black hair. The drifting mist of rain outside had left his hair damp and silken to the touch.

Behind the spinning wonder of his kiss, the recesses of her mind knew it couldn't last.

The knowledge that Wade belonged to someone else made her hungry response more desperate, savoring every fragment of the stolen embrace.

The driving possession of his mouth bent her backward while the large hand on her spine forced the lower half of her body against him. His muscled legs were hardwood columns, solid and unyielding.

The wideness of the shirt's collar made the neckline plunge to the valley between her breasts. With masterful ease he unfastened the single obstructing top button. His hand slid inside to mold itself to the mature curves of her breast, swallowing its fullness in the large cup of his hand.

Maggie shuddered with intense longing. His searing caress burned her already heated flesh.

The male smell of him was a stimulant more potent than any drug. Her heart was beating so wildly that she couldn't think.

Wade ended his imprisonment of her mouth, leaving her lips swollen with passion, and began a sensuous exploration of her curving neck. Desire quivered along her spine as he found the pleasure points that excited her, and Maggie couldn't stop the moan of delight from escaping her throat.

The fanning warmth of his disturbed breathing caressed her skin.

"God help me, Maggie, but I want you."

His husky, grudging admission sent tremors through her limbs.

She felt the pressure of his growing need for her. It was echoed by the empty ache in her loins. There was only here and now; nothing else existed, and this moment would never come again.

"Don't you think I feel the same, Wade?" she whispered.

With blazing sureness his mouth sought her lips. There was only one ultimate climax to the crushing embrace. But before a move could be made in that direction, a young voice jolted them back to reality.

"Mom! Dad! Look at the size of the fish I caught!" Mike's excited cry tore their kiss apart.

Almost immediately he came tumbling down the steps, holding the fish aloft.

There was no time for Wade to withdraw his arms from around her. A trembling Maggie was glad of their support.

Her head dipped to hide behind the protective shield of Wade's wide shoulders, concealing her love-drugged expression from her son.

She felt Wade take a deep, controlling breath before glancing over his shoulder.

"It's the biggest one yet!"

Instead of holding the fish by the gills, Mike was trying to hold it in his hands. It slipped through his grasp onto the cabin floor, giving both of them a momentary reprieve from his gaze.

"It is a big fish," Wade agreed.

"See it, mom?"

This time Mike picked it up correctly.

A supporting arm remained around her as Wade moved to one side.

"It's a beauty, Mike." Even to her own ears, her voice sounded strange.

It earned her a curious look from Mike. "Are you all right, mom?"

"I'm fine."

Maggie shivered in late reaction.

"She's just a bit chilled, that's all," Wade inserted.

Chilled. It was directly the opposite. Her whole body was suffused with heat, the heat of regret, of shame, and of love.

But Maggie didn't contradict his statement, letting it be an explanation of why Wade had been so obviously holding her.

Mike seemed satisfied with the answer and let his

attention return to the fish he held. "Actually I caught it on your pole, mom." He grinned at Wade. "I guess we'll have to say it's hers."

"I guess we will." Wade nodded in concession.

"I'd better go put this guy on the stringer and see if anything's biting on my line."

As quickly as he had come, Mike left, scurrying back on deck.

His departure left an uncomfortable void. Aware of Wade's piercing study, Maggie turned away from it. Her emotions were still too close to the surface. A bubbling sound provided the necessary distraction.

"The water's boiling," she said. "I'd better get that coffee before it boils away."

She turned her back on him as she shut off the gas to the burner.

"Maggie . . . ."

She could hear the beginnings of an apology in his voice.

No doubt it would be followed by a reminder that he was engaged to someone else and that the desire they had shared moments ago was all a mistake, and they were the very last things she wanted to hear. The tears weren't that far away.

Maggie sought refuge behind the excuse Wade had offered the last time.

"We were following the pattern of a memory, first arguing, then kissing. It didn't mean anything." *Not to you*, her heart qualified the last statement.

There was a long silence that left her with the uncanny feeling that Wade didn't believe she meant what she said. Then a drawer opened beneath one of the bunk beds.

"After you drink your coffee, it probably wouldn't hurt if you wrapped up in a blanket and stayed below."

"I think I will."

Maggie didn't fight his suggestion.

There was another pause before she heard Wade mounting the steps to the deck.

Her hand shook as she added the boiling water to the brown crystals in the mug. Now she did feel cold, and terribly lonely.

Carrying the mug to the bed, she wrapped herself in the blanket Wade had laid on the bunk.

Within minutes after she had curled herself into a ball of abject misery, Maggie heard the engines start. She knew Wade wasn't going to look for another fishing hole; he was returning to the marina. She closed her eyes and tried to forget.

Maggie didn't emerge from the cocoon of the blanket until the boat was docked, the mooring lines tied, and the engines silent.

She wadded her wet clothes into a bundle and started up the steps.

The instant she set foot on deck, Wade's voice barked, "Where do you think you're going?"

"I presume you're taking us home." His tone instantly put Maggie on the defensive. Poised short of the top step, she lifted her chin.

"Not dressed like that."

Wade softened his tone, but it was no less lacking in determination.

"I hope you don't think I'm going to wear these." She indicated the wet bundle of clothes in her hand. "They're wet. It may not bother you, but I'm not going to stain the upholstery in that expensive car by wearing these wet things."

He stood in her path, blocking it as effectively as a tall gate.

"You're not wearing that shirt."

"For heaven's sake, Wade—" his attitude rankled "—this shirt covers more than if I were wearing a bathing suit."

"I don't care how much it covers." There was a hardening set to his jaw. "No wife of mine is going to parade down these docks half-dressed."

His statement seared through her, but Maggie realized that Wade was unaware of what he had said. The swift rush of heat was quickly replaced by a chilling depression.

Avoiding his gaze, she made a bitterly mocking reply. "I'm not your wife anymore. Or had you forgotten?"

Out of the corner of her eye, she saw the startled jerk of his head. Taking advantage of the moment, she climbed the last step and brushed past him. Wade didn't try to stop her.

Mike was on the dock, standing by one of the mooring lines.

"Are you taking us straight home, dad? What about the fish?" He had seen them talking, but hadn't heard the substance of their conversation.

"Your mother needs some dry clothes," Wade answered. "As for the fish, we'll take them with us."

"You'll help me clean them, won't you? I'm still not very good at it." Mike scrambled back aboard to get the fish.

Maggie heard Wade agree as she stepped ashore. Within minutes the three of them were making their way

to the silver Mercedes in the marina parking lot. Most of
the looks that Maggie received focused on the bare length
of her legs, rather than the oversized flannel shirt and what
was, or wasn't, beneath it. Maggie ignored the mostly
admiring glances, but it wasn't so easy to ignore Wade's
growing aloofness.

At the house, Maggie carried her wet clothes to the
utility room while Mike and Wade gathered what they
needed from the kitchen to clean the fish. As they walked
out the side door to the backyard, Maggie went to her
bedroom to dress.

When they returned to the kitchen with the cleaned fish
in a pan of water, they were laughing about something. A
pain of loss and regret splintered through Maggie and she
turned away to conceal it.

Mike came rushing forward. "Will you cook the fish
tonight?"

"If you like," she agreed, taking the pan from him and
setting it on the counter.

"Great!" With her agreement obtained, he turned back
to his father. "Now we can eat what we caught, like real
outdoorsmen."

"You can."

"Aren't you staying?" Mike was surprised, but Maggie wasn't.

"I can't. I have a date tonight." Wade's voice was
smooth, his words cutting.

"But—" Mike searched for a protest "—this morning
before mom agreed to come along, you said we might not
get home until dark and we'd eat somewhere before you
brought me home. Why can't you stay now?"

He was standing close to her. Maggie turned and

quickly but affectionately placed her hand across his mouth, silencing him before his innocent remarks made the situation more awkward than it already was.

"Your father said he had to leave, Mike. That's final." She took her hand away and saw the resigned droop of his mouth.

"I'm sorry, Mike. I'll be busy tomorrow, but I'll call you Thursday," Wade promised.

"I have baseball practice in the morning," Mike told him.

"I'll remember. Between now and Thursday afternoon, you can be thinking about what you'd like to do," Wade suggested.

"Okay," Mike agreed with halfhearted enthusiasm.

The exchange was prolonged for a few more minutes before Wade finally left.

Maggie's only acknowledgment from him was a curt nod of goodbye. She turned to the sink when the door closed and began rinsing the fish in cold water. Mike watched.

"You know where he's going, don't you?" Mike said glumly.

"Where?"

"He's got a date with *her*." The feminine pronoun was emphasized with scorn as Mike wandered away from the sink.

CHAPTER ELEVEN

MAGGIE WIPED THE PERSPIRATION from her forehead with the back of her gloved hand. She hadn't realized there were so many weeds in the flower bed when she'd started. The muscles in her back were beginning to cramp from constantly bending over. But she was almost done. Arching her shoulders briefly to ease the stiffness, she again stooped to her task.

A car turned into the driveway. Her backward glance recognized the station wagon as being familiar, but she couldn't immediately decide why.

Her brows drew together in a frown as she straightened up.

The passenger door opened and Mike scrambled out, baseball and glove in his hand. "You forgot to pick me up, didn't you?" he accused.

Her green eyes widened in disbelief. "Practice can't be over this soon?"

"Well, it is," he declared in disgust. "Coach gave me a ride home since you didn't show up."

Embarrassed, Maggie glanced at the bronzed man sliding out from behind the wheel of the car.

"I'm sorry, I honestly didn't realize it was so late. I started weeding the garden and lost all track of time, I guess."

"That's all right. Things like that happen." Smiling away her apology, Tom Darby walked around the hood of the car toward her.

"All the time," Mike mumbled, but thankfully not loud enough for Tom to hear.

Denny, the neighbor boy, called to Mike, wanting him to come over. With his coach there, Mike refused, shouting, "Later!"

"Denny has a new puppy he wants you to see," Maggie told him.

"Oh!" That changed things.

He shoved his baseball and glove into her hands and raced off.

Self-conscious about her oversight, Maggie tried to make amends.

"Thanks for bringing Mike home. I really appreciate it. I know it was out of your way."

"It was no trouble at all," Tom insisted. "In fact, it gave me the perfect excuse to see you again."

His boldness took her by surprise. It shouldn't have, she realized. Her actions in the past had encouraged him to show this interest.

It was just in the last few days all her thoughts had been concerned with Wade. Tom Darby had ceased to exist in her mind as anything but Mike's coach.

"Oh." It was a small sound, revealing Maggie's inner confusion.

The initial attraction she had felt toward Tom had faded into insignificance in the face of the overwhelming emotion that consumed her. How could she handle the change?

Tom appeared not to notice her hesitation. He contin-

ued with the confidence of a man whose suit had never
been rejected. His hazel eyes looked steadily into her
green ones.

"I would like you to have dinner with me one night this
weekend. Friday or Saturday night, whichever is convenient for you?"

His technique was excellent, not giving her a chance to
say no, only to choose which night to accept.

"I'm sorry, but I really can't say if I can come."
Maggie stalled for a moment. "With Mike's father here,
it's difficult for me to make plans until I know what his
are. I'll have to take a raincheck on the invitation."

"Whatever you say." He wasn't happy with her answer, but he seemed resigned to it. Glancing up at the
clear, blue sky overhead, he remarked, "It's going to be
warm today."

Maggie sensed a hint behind the comment. Regardless
of his motives, Tom had done her a favor by bringing
Mike home.

The least she could do was repay him with some measure of hospitality.

"It's already warm. And you've been on the ball field
with those boys all morning. Let me offer you something
cold to drink since I can't accept your dinner invitation.
Iced tea, beer, Coke?"

"A beer would taste good if it isn't too much trouble,"
Tom accepted with alacrity.

"It's no trouble. I'll get it."

Tom followed her into the house, something Maggie
hadn't planned on, but she didn't object. She set Mike's
ball and glove on the kitchen table and paused to remove
her cotton work gloves.

Tom strolled along a few paces behind her, seeming to appear perfectly at home. She walked to the refrigerator.

"How is Mike doing?"

Maggie sought to establish a less personal topic of conversation, discuss Tom's work and steer away from his social life and whether it would or would not include her.

"He's doing fine, shows a real aptitude for the game."

As she opened the refrigerator door, she cast him a brief, smiling look.

"Except for his hitting, which is abominable. He was really upset that he didn't get a single hit in the game the other night."

"His hitting will improve before the summer is over," Tom replied with a certainty that revealed a firm belief in his teaching prowess. "Mike has to learn to keep his eye on the ball and stop swinging blindly at anything that comes over the plate."

"It must take a lot of patience to teach inexperienced boys how to play baseball."

Along with the can of beer, Maggie took the pitcher of iced tea from the refrigerator shelf. "Would you like a glass for your beer?"

"The can is fine."

He took it from her and pulled off the tab. "I suppose it does require patience, but the end results are rewarding. I enjoy sports and I enjoy working with kids. For me, it's natural to combine the two."

"That's good."

Taking a glass from the cupboard, Maggie filled it with tea from the pitcher for herself.

"Listen, Maggie . . . there isn't any reason why I can't bring Mike home after practice. You don't need to keep making special trips to pick him up."

He walked over to stand next to her, leaning a hip against the counter edge.

"It's very generous of you to offer, but I couldn't let you do it."

Maggie shook her head in refusal.

The sunshine streaming in through the window above the sink glinted on the fiery sheen of her hair.

It caught Tom's attention and he reached out to touch it as an innocent child would .each out for a dancing flame.

"Your hair is an extraordinary shade of red." A lock trailed across his finger. His voice was musing and absent. "Beautiful."

"Thank you." Maggie would have moved to the side to elude his involuntary caress, but the kitchen door leading outside opened.

She froze as Wade crossed the threshold and stopped, his gaze narrowing darkly, slashing from her to Tom. The curling strand of hair slid off Tom's finger. They were standing so close together at that moment that the scene didn't look as innocent as it had been: the hard glitter in Wade's eyes told Maggie that.

"Mike is at the neighbors'." Maggie took the step from Tom's side.

Her head assumed a defiant angle; she was irritated by the criticism and condemnation she saw written in Wade's features. She was single, thus free to have male friends.

"I know." Wade's attitude continued to be silently

intimidating. "I saw him when I drove in and he told me you were in the house. I wanted to speak to you."

Again, Maggie thought, and mentally braced herself. The last time he had wanted to speak to her privately it was to announce his marriage plans.

What was it about this time? Something equally shattering, she was sure.

Tom took the rather broad hint that his presence wasn't welcome and set his can of beer on the counter top.

"I'd better be moving along. Thanks for the beer, Maggie."

"I'll walk you to the door."

She had an unreasoning desire to postpone the inevitable conversation with Wade, if only for a few minutes. "Help yourself to something cold to drink, Wade. I'll be right back."

There was no response, but she hadn't expected there to be one.

Ignoring the side door Wade had entered, she led Tom through the living room to the front door.

"Thanks again for bringing Mike home."

"Maggie—" he paused at the door, his thoughtfully curious gaze resting on her face "—is there a reconciliation in the works between the two of you?"

"No, hardly," she answered with a bitterly rueful twist to her mouth.

"Are you sure? Because I had the distinct impression when he walked in that I was being confronted by an outraged husband." His head tipped skeptically at an angle.

"You must have been mistaken."

If Tom hadn't, it was probably a case that even if

Wade didn't want her anymore, he didn't want her to be with anyone else, either.

"I don't know . . . ." Tom was still hesitant.

"I do." Maggie smiled. "You see, Wade is engaged. The wedding is this month."

He seemed to digest the information before accepting it.

"I guess I did make a mistake, then." He shrugged the incident away. "I'll be seeing you, Maggie."

"Yes. Goodbye, Tom."

When he had left, Maggie returned to the kitchen. Wade had helped himself to a glass of tea and was putting the pitcher back in the refrigerator.

"Was he one of the marital prospects on your horizon?" Wade asked.

Pride made her answer, "He could be," although she seriously doubted it.

Maggie picked up her glass, glad to have something to do with her hands to hide her apprehension about this conversation.

"I'm sorry if I interrupted anything," he offered.

"No, you're not," she retorted. "If you were, you would have suggested that we talk another time and left." But she didn't confirm or deny his suspicions about the scene he had interrupted.

"What I came to discuss with you is important. I didn't think it was wise to put it off." Wade didn't defend his insincere apology.

"I'm sure it's important by *your* standards, but I might not think so."

"It's about Mike, and unless I'm greatly mistaken, he's always important to you."

It was almost a challenge.

The subject concerned Mike again, Maggie thought, the same as the last time. She didn't like the sound of it any more than the portentous feelings that made her so uneasy.

"Yes, Mike is important," she agreed warily. "What about him?"

"He hasn't met Belinda yet. Naturally she's very anxious to meet him," he said.

"Naturally."

Her voice was dry, tinged with cynicism, and it drew her a sharp look from Wade.

"I want to arrange something for this weekend."

"Fine," Maggie nodded. "Feel free to have Mike whichever day suits you best. You know I'm not going to make any objections."

"It isn't as simple as that." Wade sighed heavily in exasperation.

"Isn't it?" Mockery twisted her mouth.

"No. I want Mike to be on familiar ground when he meets her. I think it's going to be difficult enough for him without it occurring on alien ground."

"It won't be easy for Belinda, either," Maggie reminded him, not liking the direction his comments were pointing.

"She's an adult, more capable of handling a difficult situation than Mike is. It's more important for the boy to feel as comfortable as possible." He pushed aside her puny obstacle.

"What is your solution?" she challenged. "I'm sure you've already thought of one."

Wade breathed out a silent laugh, his mouth quirking cynically.

"Why do I have the feeling that the minute I answer that question this kitchen is going to turn into a battle-field?"

"Maybe because you already know I'm not going to like it."

Her nerves were tensing, her fingers tightening their grip on the moist glass, its coolness matching the temperature of her blood.

Wade held her gaze, refusing to let her look away.

"I want to bring Belinda over here to meet Mike. He would be here, in his own home, where he would be comfortable and relatively relaxed, and it would give you an opportunity to meet her at the same time. Your presence would also ease some of the pressure Mike might feel."

She didn't want that woman in her home. "You can't be serious?"

"I'm very serious."

"I can see it now, the four of us sitting around with our hands in our laps staring at each other." Maggie laughed aloud at the thought, but she didn't think it was funny, only preposterous.

"Granted, it may be awkward. It's bound to be no matter when or where it takes place," he argued, then suggested, "perhaps it would be better if we came for dinner."

"Dinner!"

"We could come in time to have a drink before we sit down to the table. There wouldn't be time for a lot of awkward silences before there'd be the distraction of the meal. Coffee afterward and then we'd leave."

"No!"

"Why?" Wade countered.

"Because . . . ."

Maggie sputtered helplessly, unable to think of an adequate reason.

"Mike has to meet her sooner or later. Why not when you're with him to lend moral support?" Wade drove home the logic of his suggestion.

But there was no one around to give her moral support, she argued silently. She sought refuge behind a weak protest.

"Mike has to meet her, but I don't!"

"Do you mean you would leave him in the care of a total stranger? Because that's exactly what you will be doing. Belinda is going to be my wife. When Mike visits me, he'll also be visiting her. Are you seriously trying to tell me you don't want to meet the woman who's going to be your son's stepmother, who'll take care of him when he's with me? I don't believe that, not for a minute."

Maggie turned away, because everything Wade had said was true.

For Mike's sake, she had to meet Wade's fiancée in order to have peace in her own mind when Mike visited Wade.

She was trapped in a corner and she resented Wade for maneuvering her there.

"Which night would you and your darling Belinda like to come for dinner?"

Cloying sarcasm rolled from her tongue, the only weapon she had left in her arsenal.

"Friday will be fine." His response was tautly controlled.

"What time?"

"Seven. There's no need to plan anything elaborate," he added.

"In other words, you don't want me to use our wedding china and crystal?" she asked sweetly.

"That attitude isn't going to make it easier," he warned.

"Easier? What do you know about making something easier?"

Her temper flared. "The only one who's finding any of this easy is you! It's going to be difficult for Mike, Belinda and myself. All you have to do is just sit back and wait for us to adjust!"

"What would you like me to do? Break the engagement?"

His look was cold, a dark brow arched in threatening challenge.

Yes! Instead Maggie cried, "No! I want you to stop telling me what my attitude should be!"

"For crissakes, I'm not telling you anything!" Wade snapped. "If you agree to my suggestion and want Belinda to dinner on Friday, then say so!"

"I do," she replied just as angrily.

"Good!"

In the next second Wade was slamming out the side door and Maggie was alone in the kitchen.

There was nothing to vent her anger on. It turned inward onto herself. Why had she baited him? What had she been trying to prove? That she was the shrew he had called her once? Why hadn't she been gracious about having Belinda to dinner? Because it hurt. The pain was agonizing.

Tension throbbed in her temples and she pressed her

fingers to them, their tips cool from holding the icy glass. The cool pressure brought temporary relief, but it came pounding back when she took her hands away. The side door opened and her head jerked up as she tried to regroup her defenses to face Wade. It was Mike who dashed in.

"Hi, mom. Dad said I was to come in and tell you I was going with him. I'll be home by five." He started back out, then paused. "Okay?"

"Yes, it's okay." She nodded with a stiff smile.

"Bye!"

CHAPTER TWELVE

MAGGIE GLANCED through the glass door of the oven to check the roast, something she had done half a dozen times in the last hour.

At the same time she checked her dim reflection in the door, an unconscious gesture to be sure her makeup didn't need retouching.

She rubbed her palms together, surprised to find them perspiring. She wiped them dry by smoothing the long black skirt over her hips.

She was nervous, her throat dry, her stomach churning. She felt like the harried image of a wife about to entertain her husband's boss—and the thought made her laugh aloud.

Mike walked into the kitchen. "What's so funny, mom?"

He wore a clean white shirt and dark blue pants. His face was scrubbed so clean that it practically shone.

"Nothing." She didn't attempt to explain the piece of irony that she had found amusing. Wade's boss was also his future father-in-law. Instead of his boss, she was about to entertain his future bride. The whole thing seemed ludicrous.

The doorbell rang. But for once Mike didn't race to answer it.

He gave her a sideways glance, and his dark eyes were filled with many of the apprehensions Maggie felt. She held out her hand to him.

"Come on, let's go and answer the door."

"I know I have to meet her," he mumbled, and moved reluctantly to walk with her, "but I wish she wasn't staying for dinner."

There wasn't any response she could make to that, so she just smiled her understanding. "Don't you feel kinda funny about meeting her?" Mike asked as they neared the front door. "I mean, because she's going to marry dad?"

"Yes, I do feel kinda funny," Maggie admitted, and that was putting it mildly.

They shared a quick smile before Maggie opened the door. She saw Wade first, standing tall and dark, dressed in a dark suit and tie, so casually elegant, and her pulse rocketed.

There was a breathless tightness in her chest. The two combined to make her feel weak at the knees.

"Hello, Maggie."

The gentle warmth in his gaze seemed to set her aglow.

"Hello, Wade." She returned the greeting with a slow smile.

Suddenly she realized this was the way she had visualized their first meeting, not the horrendous episode with hair curlers and old robe that had occurred. This was how she had imagined it—seeing each other and having the bitterness of their divorce fade under the mounting pleasure the reunion brought.

There was a movement by his side that compelled her

attention, and her gaze focused on a stunningly attractive blonde.

Belinda Hale was exactly as Maggie had pictured her to be, tall and willowy, her fairness a perfect complement to Wade's darkness.

Her hair was an unusual, and natural, shade of creamy toast, worn long and caught in a clasp at the back of her neck.

Every elegant bone reeked of smooth sophistication and poise. Her eyes were as blue as a clear Seattle sky, their color accentuated by the dress she wore in a subtle blue print.

There was only one thing about her that Maggie had not guessed—her age. *Woman* seemed a premature term. At the very most, Maggie suspected Belinda might be twenty-two.

It had never occurred to her that Wade might choose someone so much younger than himself for his future bride.

It was more disbelief than shock that kept her silent.

Belinda Hale had no such difficulty finding her voice. "Maggie, I've been looking forward to meeting you," she declared with husky sincerity and offered her hand.

Maggie managed the handshake. "How do you do, Miss Hale."

She knew she would never be able to carry off a first-name greeting, so she didn't try. In comparison to Belinda's friendliness, she knew she sounded stiff and polite. "Won't you come in?"

Moving out of the doorway, she nearly stepped into Mike, who had managed to stay well in the background and silently observe his future stepmother. Now it was his turn to be thrust into the limelight.

"You have to be Michael," Belinda deduced. "What does everyone call you? Mike or Mickey?"

He cringed at "Mickey" and quickly told her it was Mike.

Then he copied Maggie and greeted her. "How do you do, Miss Hale."

"Please call me Belinda."

She shook hands with him while Wade looked on. "You look so much like your father, Mike, I think I would have recognized you anywhere." Her gaze swung adoringly to Wade. "He's a handsome boy. No wonder you're so proud of him."

Mike shifted uncomfortably at this praise from a stranger. Maggie tried to rescue him and wondered why Wade hadn't. Was he going to leave all the conversation up to the three of them?

Of course, Belinda seemed to have enough poise to overcome any awkward silence.

"Please come into the living room and sit down." She moved toward the collection of sofas and chairs. "What can I get you to drink?" She threw a dagger at Wade for his silence. "You still drink Scotch and water, don't you?"

"Yes."

He inclined his head in agreement, nonplussed by her irritation.

"And you, Miss Hale?" Maggie inquired, and was stunned to hear herself add, "Mike is having a Coke. Would you like the same?" as if Belinda weren't old enough to drink.

The blonde seemed to miss the subtle insult, although Wade hadn't. His gaze narrowed dangerously, and Maggie knew it was a remark he wouldn't soon forget.

She bit down on her tongue and hoped she could control it.

"A glass of white wine would be nice, if you have it," Belinda answered.

"Of course."

This time Maggie was properly demure and didn't attach anything to her reply. "Make yourself at home. I'll be back in a moment."

As she started for the kitchen, Wade separated himself from Belinda's side.

"I'll help you. Mike can entertain Belinda for a few minutes."

Startled by his unexpected offer of assistance, Maggie stopped. Mike cast her a beseeching look, partly accusing her of deserting him in the face of the enemy.

But before Maggie could attempt to help him, Wade's hand was on her elbow, propelling her toward the kitchen. She didn't attempt to twist out of his hold until the door was swinging shut behind them and they were out of view.

"You left her slightly in the lurch out there," she accused.

"I think Belinda and Mike can survive for a few minutes on their own." He knew her concern wasn't for his fiancée.

Irritated, Maggie walked to the cupboard for the glasses. "The Scotch is—"

"I know where the Scotch is," he interrupted.

Pink warmed her cheeks as she remembered it hadn't

been very many days ago that he had drunk from the bottle.

She walked to the refrigerator and took out the chilling wine, as well as a Coke for Mike. Wade followed to get ice from the freezer compartment.

"Well?"

The cubes made a clinking sound as he dropped them in his glass.

"Well, what?" she retorted.

"Out with it."

"With what?" Maggie continued to be deliberately obtuse.

"It's tripping all over the tip of your tongue. You might as well say it and get it out of your system." Wade poured a shot of Scotch over the ice cubes while Maggie filled the wineglasses.

She debated silently with herself, then finally abandoned her pretended ignorance.

"When you were listing all of Belinda's virtues, you didn't mention her youth."

"She'll be twenty-two next month. It doesn't classify her as being fresh from the crib."

"But you have to admit, Wade, that Mike is closer to her age than you are."

It sounded so catty that Maggie wished she hadn't said it.

"It might make it easier for her to relate to him, and vice versa. Is her age the only objection you have to her?" he questioned.

"It wasn't an objection." She rushed to correct that assumption. "It just took me by surprise to discover she was so young. I expected her to be older, more mature. It didn't occur to me you would be attracted to a . . . woman so young."

"Why not? You were younger than Belinda is when we were married."

Her fingers trembled as she recorked the wine bottle. She didn't want to be reminded of their marriage, since it also reminded her of their regrettable divorce. Without responding to his comment, she returned the wine bottle to the refrigerator, conscious of his hooded gaze watching her.

"In many ways Belinda is more mature than you are. Her head is squarely on her shoulders. She's practical and logical in her relationships with other people. I suppose you could describe her as sensible," he concluded.

"How very dull," was Maggie's first reaction, and naturally she said it.

"After our tumultuous years, I think it will be a refreshing change of pace to be married to Belinda." His retort was quick and intended to cut.

"I hope the two of you will be very comfortable together."

She arranged the glasses on a serving tray. "Now, Belinda may not need rescuing, but I think Mike does. Shall we go back to the living room?"

"After you. And, Maggie—" the hard line of his mouth was tempered by forced patience "—try to hold your tongue."

"I do try, Wade. Believe me, I do," she said, taking a deep breath and picking up the tray.

Maggie had expected their return would be met with a searching look. In Belinda's place, she would have been curious and a little jealous to have Wade alone in the

kitchen with his ex-wife. But there wasn't a trace of either
emotion in the blonde's smiling look. Belinda was either
very understanding or very confident that Wade loved
only her.

"I hope we didn't take too long." Maggie felt their
return demanded some remark from her as hostess, then
immediately realized the words she had chosen might
intimate that they had been doing more in the kitchen than
fixing the drinks.

And after she had just promised Wade she would watch
what she said!

She felt doomed.

"Not at all." Belinda seemed indifferent to their ab-
sence. She smiled at Wade as he sat on the sofa cushion
beside her. "Mike and I have been talking about different
things."

"Oh?"

Maggie glanced at Mike. He didn't look as if he'd been
doing very much talking. But she felt a curiosity for their
subject. "What about?"

Belinda answered, "He was telling me about the fishing trip the three of you took this week. He said each of
you caught a fish."

"That isn't exactly true," Maggie corrected the impression, and wondered if Wade hadn't mentioned that she
had accompanied him and Mike. "I didn't actually catch a
fish. Mike caught one on my rod and gave me credit for
it."

"You would have caught it," he came to her defense,
"if you hadn't fallen overboard."

"You fell overboard?" The blonde's expression was
all concern.

Maggie wished Mike hadn't offered that piece of information.

"Yes. It was really nothing."

"How did it happen?"

"Mom caught this fish," Mike started to explain, "and she couldn't get the hook out of its mouth, so dad had to do it for her. He said it was too small to keep and they started arguing."

Maggie wished he wouldn't go into such detail, but there didn't seem to be any way to stop him. "When dad tossed it back into the water, mom tried to catch it. She slipped and went headfirst over the side. Dad tried to grab her, but all he got was her shoe. It was the funniest thing you ever saw!"

Mike was beginning to smile at the memory.

In retrospect, Maggie could see the humor of the incident.

"Mom was soaking wet when she climbed back on the boat. She really got mad when she saw me and dad laughing at her," Mike confided. "When dad gave her the tennis shoe he'd grabbed off her foot, she threw it in the water. I hooked it with my line and got it back before it sank."

"You didn't laugh at her, did you, Wade?" Belinda glanced at him with reproach.

"I'm afraid I did," he admitted, a devilish, unapologetic light dancing in his dark eyes.

"That wasn't kind. No wonder you lost your temper, Maggie," Belinda sympathized.

"I imagine I looked pretty comical."

Maggie found herself defending their amusement at her expense.

"You looked even funnier in that shirt," Mike piped up.

"What shirt?" Belinda asked.

"All her clothes were wet, so mom had to wear this shirt. Only it was too big for her," Mike explained.

"How awful for you, Maggie! It must have been a trying experience."

Again Maggie dismissed the offer of sympathy. "Now that I'm warm and dry and on land, I've recovered my sense of humor. Looking back, it doesn't seem quite so bad."

"Do you like to fish, Miss Hale?" Mike wanted to know.

"Call me Belinda," she corrected him. "Yes, I do like to fish. Wade has taken me with him several times in Alaska. When you come to visit us, the three of us will have to go fishing together."

"It could be fun, huh?" Mike seemed to consider the possibility.

"Not the same kind of fun as you have with your mother." Belinda was making an attempt to show she didn't intend to try to take Maggie's place—a commendable gesture. "At least, I hope I don't fall into the river," she joked. "The water up there is very cold."

"I wouldn't worry about that." Wade's arm was draped over the back of the sofa, lightly brushing the girl's shoulders.

The affection in the implied caress sent a wave of jealousy through Maggie. "There's only one Maggie. The things that happen to her aren't likely to happen to anyone else."

"Thank heaven!" Her murmured response was dryly

sarcastic, directed at Wade. His barbed look made her cover it. "Do you ski, Miss Hale? With all that snow in Alaska, it would be a shame if you didn't."

"I love to ski. Of course, there are times when it's too bitterly cold to be out in it."

"I'm sure that's true, but what a perfect excuse to drape yourself in furs."

Maggie sipped at her wine, hating the image of the young blonde wrapped in sables.

"Oh, no, I never wear animal fur," Belinda denied that thought. "I can't stand the idea of an animal being killed just so its fur can be used for a coat."

Good heavens, doesn't she have any faults, Maggie wondered in irritation.

She didn't seem human. Even now, confronted by Wade's ex-wife, Belinda was gracious and charming and disgustingly friendly.

"Oh, dear," Maggie heard herself murmuring with false concern, "I do hope you're not a vegetarian. I have a beautiful rib roast cooking in the oven."

Belinda just laughed at the comment, a throaty, genuinely amused sound.

"No, I'm not a vegetarian. My concern for animal life doesn't seem to apply to my stomach. Or maybe it's the practical side of me that abhors waste. I've never been able to understand why people in India have to starve when there are all those sacred cattle roaming around. It's so senseless and tragic."

"Yes, I know what you mean." But Maggie had the feeling she had lost another round. She set her wineglass down. "Excuse me, I think I'd better check on the dinner."

"May I help?" Belinda offered.

"She's an excellent cook," Wade inserted, smiling when Belinda beamed at his compliment.

"I don't doubt it," was Maggie's slightly snappish reply of jealousy. Again she masked it with a quick smile. "Thank you, but I can manage. Excuse me."

CHAPTER THIRTEEN

IN THE KITCHEN she wanted to bang pots and pans, slam cupboard doors, release all this pent-up frustration. How could anyone possibly compete with a woman who was so perfect?

She forced herself to control the anger she felt, but it seethed inside her, bubbling like a volcano.

To make her feel worse, she didn't think there was a gram of jealousy in Belinda's body.

She herself was torn apart by the emotion, and it made her feel small and mean.

When she was satisfied that everything was in order in the kitchen, Maggie decided it was better to begin dinner now than wait and risk overcooking the meal. She carried the servings of spinach salad to the dining-room table before returning to the living room to suggest they come to the table.

"Spinach salad, one of my favorites," Belinda remarked as she sat in a chair opposite from Wade. "Did you tell her it was?" she asked him, and Maggie immediately wished she had chosen something else for the salad course.

"No, I didn't mention it to her."

"It's one of our favorites," Maggie explained grudgingly.

"Do you like spinach, Mike?"

Belinda smiled at the dark-haired boy sitting at the head of the table.

"I like it this way, but I don't like it when it's cooked."

"I don't think many children do," Belinda replied with understanding.

Maggie suspected she was a veritable paragon of understanding. "This is a beautiful set of china, Maggie."

"A wedding gift." Now why had she volunteered that information, Maggie wondered. Why hadn't she simply accepted the compliment with a thank-you? Her irritation increased.

"Are you and dad going to have kids?" Mike blurted out the question.

Maggie felt her cheeks flame in an attempt to match the color of her hair, but she was the only one who registered any embarrassment. Belinda seemed to find nothing wrong with it.

Wade shot Maggie a look that seemed to accuse her of somehow instigating the question.

"We want to have a family, yes," Belinda answered. "We both love children and hope to have several babies. What do you think about becoming a big brother?"

"I don't know."

Mike shrugged and attacked his salad.

Maggie's fork extracted vengeance from the innocent green leaves. Several babies. One big happy family. The only thing wrong with the picture was that Belinda would be in her place. The need to destroy the image consumed her.

"Are you sure you want to go through the two-o'clock

feedings, the croup and teething again, Wade?'' She hid her jealousy behind taut mockery. ''Don't you think you're getting a bit old for that? You should have children when you're young and your nerves are more capable of taking the strain. Of course, Belinda is still young and can handle it, but you . . . .'' Maggie let the sentence trail away unfinished, again drawing attention to their age difference.

There was a dangerous glitter in his dark eyes, but Wade responded with marked evenness. ''I'm certain I'll be able to cope, Maggie.''

''I think Wade will make an excellent father,'' Belinda remarked. ''But I suppose you've already had proof of that.''

Again, it was a calm statement of fact, with no envy.

''Wade was a very good father, and still is,'' Maggie agreed, mimicking the blonde's tone. ''I was only concerned that when your children are grown, Wade will practically be in his dotage.''

''What's dotage?'' Mike frowned.

''It's a diplomatic way of saying 'old age,' '' Wade explained, his mouth twisted wryly. ''Your mother is trying to point out that I'm getting older.''

''You are old, aren't you?'' Mike countered with perfect innocence.

It was all Maggie could do not to laugh.

Wade managed to maintain his composure, however tightly held. ''I prefer to believe that I'm just approaching my prime.''

''That's so very true in our society.'' Belinda expanded on his answer.

"A man's attraction increases when he's over thirty, but when a woman reaches that age, she's considered over the hill. I think it's terribly unfair. But haven't you found it to be true, Maggie?"

She was so outraged she couldn't speak.

It didn't matter that the remark hadn't been intended to be personal. It was an unnecessary reminder of her own age.

Wade recognized the danger signals flashing from her. "That opinion is changing. Women over thirty are still very desirable, and people are beginning to recognize that."

He salved her wounded ego.

Maggie had never been particularly sensitive about her age until that moment. Despite Wade's comment, she still felt slightly raw. She managed to bring her temper down to a low simmer. Maggie used the excuse that she had to bring the rest of the food from the kitchen in order to make a discreet exit and regain control of her turbulent emotions.

As she transferred the meat from its roasting pan onto a platter, she realized Wade hadn't said that for her sake. He had been protecting his fiancée from the scorching flash of her temper.

How stupid of her not to have guessed!

The heat of her anger increased a degree instead of lowering.

Maggie laid the carving knife and fork on the meat platter and carried it into the dining room, where she set it in front of Wade.

"Will you carve the meat?"

"Yes," he agreed, and eyed her with quiet speculation.

Gathering the salad plates, she carried them to the kitchen.

With an ominously steady hand she dished up the potatoes and vegetables to take them in.

Over and over in her mind she kept repeating that she wouldn't lose her temper no matter how sorely she was tried.

"Maggie, I think the relationship you have with Mike is quite remarkable," Belinda declared.

"Oh? Why is that?" She set the bowl of potatoes beside Mike's plate.

"I believe it's difficult to raise an only child, especially when the parents are divorced. The tendency for a single parent is to become overprotective. Yet Mike shows no signs of that, even though you are very close. I think it's marvelous that it's turned out that way, since you're nearing the age where it isn't wise to have more children."

There was absolutely nothing malicious in the comment, but it struck a nerve that had become touchy. It was sheer misfortune that Maggie was standing beside Belinda's chair when she made it.

And it was even worse that she had a bowl of cream peas and pearl onions in her hand.

With no conscious direction from her mind, her hand tipped the bowl and poured the creamy vegetables in Belinda's lap. The instant she heard the other girl's startled shriek and saw what she had done, Maggie was horrified.

"I'm so sorry! I don't know how it happened." She was grabbing for a napkin as Belinda pushed her chair away from the table.

"I'm sorry," she repeated, and dabbed ineffectually at the spreading stain of cream sauce and smashed peas.

"Damn you, Maggie!"

Wade was swearing under his breath and pushing her out of the way. "I should have known something like this would happen!"

While it hadn't been exactly deliberate, Maggie didn't try to protest her innocence. She wasn't entirely convinced herself that it had been an accident. She felt wretched.

Belinda recovered sufficiently from her stunned dismay to murmur, "It's all right. I'm sure it was an accident."

Maggie thought she would have felt better if the young woman had yelled abuse at her.

All this magnanimous forgiving and understanding was becoming too much.

Mike wasn't helping matters. Both hands were clamped over his mouth in an attempt to hold back his convulsing laughter.

One glance at Maggie and Mike turned away, his shoulders shaking all the harder.

"Come on, Belinda."

Wade was helping the girl to her feet. The worst of the cream sauce and peas were absorbed and blobbed on a once white napkin.

But they had left a large, ugly stain down the front of the blue dress. "I'll take you home," he told her.

"I'm sorry," Maggie repeated, helpless to undo what she had done.

"It will clean, don't worry," Belinda assured her, still slightly in a daze.

"Please send me the bill," Maggie insisted as she followed the couple to the front door. "I'll pay for it."

"You're damned right you will!" Wade snapped. And Maggie knew he wasn't talking about money.

"It was nice meeting you," Belinda called over her shoulder as Wade hustled her out the door.

That convinced Maggie the girl wasn't human. No ordinary mortal could have a bowl of peas spilled on her and still say with sincerity that it was nice to meet the person who did it.

Maggie walked numbly back into the dining room and stared at the peas and onions on the carpet beside Belinda's chair.

Mike no longer tried to contain his laughter as tears rolled from his eyes.

"Stop laughing, Mike! It isn't funny."

"Yes, it is. It's the funniest thing I ever saw!"

"Just shut up and help me clear up this mess before the peas get ground into the carpet."

Maggie bent down and began picking up the vegetables drenched in cream sauce.

Mike joined her, wiping the tears from his cheeks and trying to choke back the laughter. "Mom," he declared, "you're priceless!"

CHAPTER FOURTEEN

MAGGIE FOLDED the damp dish towel and hung it on its rack to dry.

Apart from the leftover roast and potatoes in the refrigerator, there was nothing about the house to suggest she had entertained guests that evening.

All the dishes were washed and put away. The carpet in the dining room had been spot-cleaned of its cream sauce.

The linen tablecloth was buried in the clothes hamper, along with the napkins.

This elimination of any hint of entertaining extended even to herself.

Her face was scrubbed clean of all makeup. The long black hostess skirt and silver lamé blouse were hanging in her closet once again. The onyx earrings were in her jewel box, and the black evening shoes were in her shoe bag.

In their place she wore her new forest green house robe. Barefoot, Maggie walked to the coffeepot and filled a cup with the fresh brew.

The doorbell rang and she didn't need a magic genie to tell her who it was. She had known all along that Wade would be coming back after he had seen Belinda safely home.

She walked into the dining room toward the living room.

Mike answered the door, as she had known he would. "Mom? Dad's here!"

Wade had not changed his clothes. But the knot of his tie was loosened and the top button of his shirt unfastened.

The small change seemed to remove the veneer of civilization to expose a ruthless quality.

As wrong as she was, Maggie wouldn't bow her head to him.

"Hello, Wade," Her voice was amazingly steady. "I've been expecting you. The coffee is fresh. Would you like a cup?"

"No."

Wade glanced at Mike, who was watching them both with silent expectancy.

"Go to your room, Mike. I want to speak to your mother in private."

"Okay."

Mike didn't argue. "Don't be too hard on her, dad. Mom feels pretty bad about what happened."

"On second thought, call your friend next door and see if you can spend the night with him," Wade told him.

Mike glanced hesitantly at Maggie. With a silent nod, she gave her permission. The strained silence over the next few minutes, during which Mike telephoned and got an invitation to spend the night with his friend, was an ordeal.

Maggie drank her coffee and tasted none of it. Both she and Wade were too tense to sit down. They wandered aimlessly around the living room like circling combatants until Mike left.

Then finally, when they were alone, they confronted each other.

Maggie took the initiative. "There's no excuse for what I did tonight," she began.

"I'm glad you realize that."

The fact that she took the blame didn't appease Wade's anger.

"I didn't do it intentionally, I swear," Maggie continued.

"It sure as hell wasn't an accident," he growled.

"It wasn't an accident, but it wasn't on purpose, either."

She set her cup down and twisted her fingers together. "I didn't even know what I was doing until it was too late."

"Why, Maggie? Why?" Wade raked his fingers through the side of his hair. "Why did you do it?"

"How should I know?" Maggie protested, angered by her helplessness to explain. "It just happened."

"Nothing 'just happens.' Not with you! You make things happen. You strike sparks, then fan them into flames. Before you know it, the fire sweeps through everything and you have a disaster on your hands."

"If you feel that way, you never should have brought her over here in the first place!" She struck back with equal vehemence.

"That's typical!" Wade declared with an angry, exasperated sigh. "Blame me because you can't control your temper."

"I'm not blaming you—I blame myself. It was unforgivable and I know that! But I just couldn't take it anymore.''

"Take what? Don't tell me you let all that talk about age get under your skin? Why should that bother you?''

"Oh, yes, I remember all you said about women over thirty still being desirable,'' Maggie said caustically. "It was nothing but talk.

"Look at you—you're marrying a twenty-year-old woman.''

"Twenty-one.''

"Twenty-one,'' she repeated. "Let's not forget that one year.''

Sarcasm coated her tongue. "It makes all the difference, doesn't it?''

"For God's sake, Maggie, I meant every word I said!'' He took her by the shoulders and shook her hard. "Haven't my actions since I came back proved that I find you a very desirable woman still?''

"I'm nothing but a habit to you!''

She flung back his words that had stung her before. "Like when a person quits smoking and keeps on wanting a cigarette.''

"Yes,'' Wade agreed tightly, "even when he knows it's bad for him.

"The problem is when he lights up a cigarette again, all he remembers is how good it is. That's how it's been for me ever since I made the mistake of kissing you again. All I can think about is how good it is.''

"Sure,'' she mocked. "That's why you're engaged to Belinda.''

"It's confusing, isn't it?'' One corner of his mouth curled in a cynical smile.

"You ought to be in my shoes if you want to know what real confusion is like. Belinda is a girl in a million, yet—"

"I don't care if she's a girl in ten million. I'm sick and tired of hearing about her!" Maggie was nearly in tears as she struggled futilely to break out of Wade's hold. "I don't want to hear about her virtues—or the children you're going to have!"

"Jealous?"

Maggie hesitated for only an instant before abandoning all pretense to the contrary. "Yes! Yes, I am jealous. I didn't want to be, I told myself I wouldn't be. But I am jealous of her!"

"Why?" His dark gaze seemed to bore deep into her very soul. "We're divorced. Remember?"

"I know that. And I know I should want you to be happy, but . . . . Why should both of us be alone and miserable?"

"Are you miserable, Maggie?" His hands tightened, drawing her a few inches closer.

Her fingers spread across his chest, slipping inside his jacket to cover the thinness of his shirt. She strained to keep him at a distance.

Conscious of the subtle change in the atmosphere, her pulse behaved erratically.

"Yes, I'm miserable," she admitted, and stared at the hairs curling near the hollow of his throat.

"Don't you like being alone?" Wade demanded.

"No."

"My independent, stubborn little Maggie doesn't like being alone?"

His faint skepticism made it a question. "That's a

change. Six years ago that was the one thing you wanted above all else.''

"I know.''

"Maggie—'' his large hand curved around her throat and under her chin, lifting it up ''—did we give up too soon? Could we have made our marriage work?''

A tear collected on the tip of her eyelash. "I don't know.''

"What do you know?''

There was a mocking lilt to his low voice that was oddly pleasing.

"I . . . I know that I'm sorry for spilling those peas all over Belinda. I never meant to do it, honestly.''

An attempt at a smile trembled over her lips. "There, you have your apology from me. Now you can go back to Belinda and tell her how very contrite I am. In a few days you'll both be laughing about what a termagant your ex-wife is.''

"I never laugh about you, Maggie. I never have.''

His hard features were composed in a serious expression.

"When we were divorced, I immediately asked my company to transfer me to Alaska because I knew I would never be able to stay away from you unless thousands of miles separated us. Each month, each year, the separation became easier to bear until finally I met Belinda.

"Then I came back here.'' Wade took a deep breath and released it in a long sigh. "And I find I still can't stay away from you.''

"It hasn't been easy to get you out of my system, either.''

Maggie was moved by his words into admitting her own impossible position.

His hands relaxed on her shoulders and slid around to cross her back. It happened so gently and without force that she barely realized she was being enfolded in his arms.

Her head rested against his shoulder. She felt the feather-light brush of his mouth against her hair, but she didn't object.

"What are we going to do about us?" he mused.

"There isn't any us."

She slid her hands the rest of the way inside his jacket to wind her arms around his middle, unconsciously hugging closer.

"Isn't there, Maggie?"

He kissed the corner of her eye.

She lifted her head and his mouth found her lips.

It was a warm, drugging kiss, slow to passion, allowing Maggie to enjoy the sensation as she moved toward the heights.

Wade was content to make the climb at a leisurely pace.

"Legally we may not be bound to each other," he murmured against the sensitive cord along her neck. "But we haven't broken that one tie that keeps pulling us back together."

"Not Mike?"

"No, not Mike."

His hands roamed with indolent ease over her slim figure, slowly but surely molding her to his granite length.

"We're like two pieces of flint, Maggie. Every time

we rub up against each other, we strike sparks. We keep forgetting to put the fire out."

"It's just physical."

Her lips began to intimately trace the outline of his jaw, so strong and firm.

"That's what I keep telling myself." Wade nibbled at the lobe of her ear. "That you just know how to please me."

"That was a long time ago."

Maggie felt her heart hammering in response to the rapid beat of his.

Her legs felt shaky and weak.

"Was it?" He moved back to nuzzle her lips. "Or was it only last night in my dreams?"

His fingers located the zipper latch in the front of her robe.

It slid slowly down to her waist, the hair-roughened back of his hand tickling her bare skin. She seemed to lose her breath as his hand slid inside.

"This is crazy, Wade. We argue all the time." But even as she made the protest, her lips were parting in anticipation of his kiss.

"We aren't having an argument now, unless you intend to start one." His mouth hovered close to hers, without taking it.

"I should." But Maggie hadn't the strength to resist, only to press her mouth to his and accept its hard possession.

Flames leaped and soared around them. Their desire melted them together.

His hands burned over her skin, arousing her flesh to the demands of his.

They were reaching the corner where there would be no turning back.

To her surprise, Maggie found herself breaking away from his kiss. She was trembling, weak with her hunger for him.

Yet she was resisting. It confused her.

"Maggie?"

His fingers sought her chin, trying to twist her head back to him.

"I can't," she answered his unspoken question.

"Why?" His bewildered demand echoed what she was feeling.

"I do want you to make love to me." Maggie looked at him at last, her heart in her eyes.

"But I can't let you. I don't understand it myself, so don't ask me to explain."

"Is it because of Belinda?"

His hand continued its caressing massage of her lower back, an unconscious motion that was sensually disturbing.

"Maybe," she conceded without knowing if it were true.

"It's just . . . that I don't want this to happen for old times' sake. I don't want tonight to be one last fling before you marry Belinda."

Although Wade didn't move, Maggie felt him withdrawing behind a wall of reserve. He was taking control of his emotions and his desires. She wasn't sure if she was glad about that or not.

"I understand," he murmured.

"Do you?" Maggie hoped he did. "We've always done things so impulsively, made decisions in the heat of the moment. Getting married, *and* getting divorced. Before we make another foolish decision, I—"

His forefinger pressed itself against her lips for silence. "Don't say any more." He smiled tightly. "I couldn't stand the shock of hearing practical, sensible statements coming from you."

With a reluctance that thrilled her, he withdrew his arms from around her and zipped the front of her robe shut all the way to her neck. Maggie stood there uncertainly, regretting that she had stopped him even though she knew she was right.

"I don't want you to go," she sighed.

His mouth crooked into a wry smile. "Don't ask me to stay and sleep on the couch."

"Okay, I won't."

She copied his smile. "You sleep in the bed and I'll take the couch."

She was joking and Wade knew it, but he answered seriously.

"I need to think, Maggie, and I can do a better job of it if I don't have the distraction of knowing you are in another room."

"You're leaving, then?"

Maggie said it almost as if she were repeating a verdict.

"Yes."

"Tomorrow . . ." she began.

Wade bent and kissed her lightly on the lips. "We'll see what tomorrow brings.

"By then we'll both have time to be sure our decision is right."

Maggie could have told him that her decision was

already made, but pride demanded that she remain silent.

A shiver of apprehension chilled her skin. What if she had missed her chance for happiness?

He walked to the door and paused, not looking back. "Good night, Maggie."

At least it hadn't been goodbye. Not yet, anyway. "Good night, Wade."

WHAT WAS SHE DOING, Maggie wondered as he opened the door and walked out into the night.

Was she sending him back into Belinda's waiting arms?

She hadn't told him that she loved him. Maybe it was better that way.

If his decision went against her, at least she could save face.

She had to accept the probability that Wade wouldn't choose her. He had to care a great deal for Belinda or he would never have asked her to marry him in the first place.

Maggie had no such choice to make. There was only Wade.

A car door slammed. Shortly afterward she heard the engine start and the car reversed out of the driveway. It was going to be a long night, the waiting turning it into an eternity.

She picked up her coffee cup and carried it to the kitchen.

She refilled it and sat down at the chrome table.

It was three in the morning before she turned off the lights and went to bed.

She lay there for a long time, staring at the pattern the moonlight made on the ceiling. At some point in the aching loneliness of time, Maggie drifted off to sleep.

CHAPTER FIFTEEN

A BELL RANG. At first Maggie thought it was her alarm clock and swung her hand to the bedside table to shut it off.

But it wasn't the alarm clock. She fumbled for the telephone, but there was a dial tone on the other end. The bell sounded again as she was about to decide she had dreamed it.

"Mike! Answer the door!" she called, and tried to bury her head under the pillow.

At this hour of the morning any visitor had to be one of Mike's friends.

Then she realized that Mike wasn't home. He had spent the night with Denny next door. And there was only one possible person who might be coming at this hour to see her.

Maggie shot out of the bed like a loaded cannon. She pulled on her robe as she raced down the hall.

"I'm coming!" she called as the doorbell rang again.

Breathless, her face aglow with excitement and hope, she pulled back the bolt and unhooked the safety chain. She jerked the door open, beaming a smile of welcome. But it wasn't Wade standing outside.

It was Belinda Hale.

Maggie stared.

The blonde looked immaculate, not a hair out of place, a sparing but efficient use of makeup. In comparison Maggie felt tousled and sleep-worn, her eyes puffy, her hair a tangle of red silk, too pale without makeup.

"May I come in?" Belinda asked.

Too startled to do anything else, Maggie stepped to one side to admit her.

"I'm a mess, I'm afraid," she apologized for her appearance. "I've just got out of bed."

"That's all right, I understand. I'm never at my best until I've had my orange juice and a morning cup of coffee." Again, there was that smooth, understanding smile.

"About last night and your dress . . ." Maggie began.

"I think we would both feel better if we just forgot about last night and that little incident," Belinda suggested. "I'm convinced you didn't do it intentionally."

"I didn't," Maggie assured her.

"You must be dying for some juice and a cup of coffee. Why don't we go into the kitchen?

"I wouldn't mind another cup myself, if it isn't too much trouble." There was nothing pushy in her manner.

On the contrary, the young woman was being very thoughtful.

"The kitchen is through here."

Maggie led the way. Her mind raced to find a reason for Belinda's arrival here this morning, but she was hesitant to ask.

"This is nice." Belinda glanced around the kitchen in

approval. "Very efficient. It must be a pleasure to cook here."

"It is, when I have the time."

Maggie quickly made a pot of coffee and plugged it in before walking to the refrigerator for the orange juice.

"Where's Mike this morning?"

Was that the reason for Belinda's visit? To renew her acquaintance with Mike? "He's next door at the neighbors'." It was logical since he hadn't yet returned home.

"That's good. It will give us a chance to have a private talk."

"Talk?"

Her hand halted in midair, the orange juice glass poised short of her mouth.

"Yes. I made sure Wade's car wasn't here before I stopped. I knew he wouldn't like me coming to talk to you."

Belinda smiled with faint conspiracy and sat down at the chrome table.

"Wade's car?" Maggie repeated.

"Please don't try to spare me. And please don't be embarrassed," the other girl insisted. "I know Wade spent the night with you last night. I'm not upset. In fact, I think it might be a good thing in the long run."

"You know Wade spent the night here with me?" Maggie repeated the statement to be certain she had heard it correctly.

"Yes. It was fairly obvious. When he took me home, I knew he was coming back here. He came back because he was upset and angry about what had happened to my dress. You're a strikingly beautiful woman, Maggie. When Wade didn't come home, I knew that whatever sparks had flown between you hadn't all been from anger,'' Belinda explained.

Maggie couldn't believe what she was hearing. "You know he made love to me and you don't mind?" She found that impossible.

"No, I don't mind." Belinda shook her blond head, her expression indulgently gentle. "You see, I think I understand what happened. When a man sees his ex-wife again, it's natural for him to wonder if that old feeling is still around."

"And last night Wade satisfied his curiosity?" Maggie was incredulous that Belinda could take the supposed defection of her fiancé so calmly.

"It's better than having him marry me and wonder about you," Belinda answered.

"Don't you think so?"

"Oh, yes, much better, I'm sure," Maggie agreed dryly, and walked to the cupboard to take out two clean mugs.

"Do you take cream or sugar?"

"Both, please."

"Have you talked to Wade this morning?" She took the sugar bowl out of the cupboard and walked to the refrigerator for the cream.

"No, he wasn't back yet when I left the house. Naturally I'm not going to tell him that I know all about last night. He may volunteer the information on his own, but I won't admit that I know. I think it's the wisest thing. I don't want him to think that I'm the possessive type and will check up on him all the time."

"You are definitely not the possessive type," Maggie agreed with the faintest trace of sarcasm.

"It's a waste of emotion. A man is either going to be faithful or he's not. A woman can do all the worrying in the world about where he is or who he's with, but it won't change anything. It can make your life miserable," Belinda declared. "And I'm not going to let my life become miserable."

"It's a commendable philosophy, but difficult to live by, I would think."

The coffeepot stopped perking and Maggie filled the cups.

"Not if you set your mind to it. It becomes amazingly easy."

There was an expressive lift to her shoulders. "It's a matter of not being distracted by harmful emotions."

"I see."

Maggie didn't see at all. By nature she was an emotional person. Belinda seemed the complete opposite. "What is it you wanted to talk to me about?" She carried the mugs to the table, set one in front of Belinda along with the cream and sugar, and carried the second to her chair.

"About Wade."

Mentally Maggie braced herself.

This was the part she understood, where Belinda would ask her to stay away from him, that he no longer belonged to her.

"What about Wade?" Maggie sipped the steaming coffee.

"I want to know all about him—the things that irritate him, the things he likes. There are so many pitfalls in a marriage. I thought if I talked to you first, I could avoid some of the major ones."

Maggie set the cup down with a jerk, brown liquid slopping over the rim.

There would be no ultimatum for her to leave Wade alone, she realized.

"You can't be serious!"

She choked on her disbelief.

"Oh, but I am. Don't you see how sensible it is?" the other girl reasoned.

"Sensible? You just accused me of having slept with your fiancé last night. Don't you realize that?" Maggie asked incredulously. "Now you're asking me to tell you all the do's and don'ts so your marriage to him can survive. I could tell you all the wrong things, deliberately."

"But you wouldn't do that, Maggie." Belinda laughed away the suggestion.

"Wade has always said that one of your greatest faults was your honesty. If anything, you have proved that to me this minute."

"Did it ever occur to you that I might want Wade back?" Maggie argued.

"Of course it occurred to me. But if there'd been any chance of a reconciliation between you, it would have happened before now."

The woman's confidence was unshakable. Belinda's total lack of jealousy put Maggie at a loss. It was impossible to be angry, or even irritated, in the face of this insanely sensible girl.

That left bewilderment.

"What if I told you Wade and I discovered that old

special feeling was still there? What would you say?''
Maggie wanted to know.

"That it's a good thing Wade found out before he
married me."

Belinda's tone indicated that that was the only logical
reaction.

Logic had never ruled Maggie's heart. She leaned back
in her chair, completely baffled.

"I give up," she sighed in helpless confusion. "You
can't be real!"

Belinda laughed, that throaty, practiced sound.

CHAPTER SIXTEEN

THE SIDE DOOR OPENED and Wade walked in.

He let the door close behind him as he stopped and a puzzling frown of disbelief spread across his male features.

His jacket and tie had been discarded, but otherwise he was wearing the same clothes he had had on last night.

There was a shadowy growth of beard on his cheeks to indicate that he hadn't shaved yet this morning. His black hair was rumpled as if he'd run his fingers through it many times.

His dark gaze narrowed on Belinda.

"I saw your car in the driveway."

His voice indicated that he hadn't believed what he'd seen.

"Our little triangle is complete now," Maggie quipped. "Sit down, Wade. Join us for a cup of coffee, although you might feel the need for something stronger."

He slid a questioning glance at her before sharply returning his attention to Belinda. "What are you doing here?"

If Belinda found the situation awkward, she didn't show it.

"I was in the neighborhood so I thought I'd stop by and assure Maggie that there was no permanent damage to my dress. I had no idea you were coming."

"When you weren't home, I had no idea you would be here, either."

His attitude was wary and suspicious, not completely accepting the surface explanation.

Maggie rose from her chair, a false smile, tinged with cynicism, curving her mouth. "I'm afraid the cat is out of the bag, darling." She walked past him to the kitchen cupboard.

"What cat? What are you talking about?" His frown darkened in confused anger.

Lack of sleep had deepened the lines in his face, highlighting his male attraction.

"Belinda knows you spent the night with me," she told him sweetly, and poured a third cup of coffee.

"She knows *what!*" Wade roared after a stunned second.

"Don't raise your voice, darling," Maggie chided him with mock reproof. "I said Belinda knows you and I were together all night. Don't worry, dear, she doesn't mind."

"Wade, I don't want you to think I was checking up on you," Belinda inserted as he was momentarily at a loss for words. "Believe me, that's the last thing I would do."

"You see?" Maggie's green eyes rounded with innocent serenity. "She does understand."

She started to hand Wade the cup of coffee and paused. "Would you like it plain, or shall I lace it with a little Scotch?"

"I'll take it plain," he snapped, and reached for the

cup. His accusing dark eyes impaled Maggie. "Perhaps you'd better explain to me what's going on? What have you been telling Belinda?"

"Me? I haven't told her anything." Mockingly Maggie placed one hand on her heart and lifted the other as if taking an oath.

Wade gritted his teeth, anger seething through. "You—"

"Don't be angry with Maggie," Belinda broke in. "She didn't tell me anything until she found out that I already knew."

"Knew what?" Wade turned roundly on the girl at the table.

"Darling, you aren't listening," Maggie taunted, and brushed past him to take her chair at the table.

He flashed her an impatient look and demanded of Belinda, "What makes you think I spent the night here?"

"It's fairly obvious, I think." Belinda shrugged. "After you left me, you came back here. And you never came home last night."

"Naturally, she reached the logical conclusion that—"

"Stay out of this, Maggie." Wade cut her short and glowered at Belinda.

"So you assumed I spent the night with Maggie. I admit I was tempted. With the right encouragement, I probably would have!"

"Oh."

For the first time, Belinda looked to be in water out of her depth.

"Then where were you?" Immediately her hand waved aside the question, indicating Wade should ignore it.

"No. No, you don't have to answer that. I don't expect you to report your every move to me. I have no intention of tying you down, or interfering in any way with the freedom of your movements."

"You certainly can't accuse Belinda of being possessive, Wade."

"Maggie!"

Wade warned her to keep silent.

"Sorry," she said with false innocence laughing in her green eyes.

"If you like, I can leave you two to thrash this out on your own."

"If there's anything that needs thrashing, it's you," he retorted.

"I feel so awful, Maggie. I owe you an apology for what I was thinking," Belinda insisted.

"No, you don't." Maggie's natural candor surfaced. "If I could live last night over again, it would probably turn out to be just the way you thought it had. Your assumption was wrong, but not because I didn't want Wade to stay.

"I did, but I was afraid one of us, or both of us, might regret it in the morning. So don't apologize. If anyone is sorry, it's me," Maggie concluded and stared into her coffee cup, all her cynical humor at the situation gone.

"Now that you have that confession out of your system," Wade declared, "I think it's time Belinda was leaving.

"Come on," he told his fiancée and helped pull her chair away from the table. "You and I have some things to discuss."

"Of course, Wade," Belinda agreed. But he wasn't giving her a chance to disagree as he took hold of her arm and forced her to walk to the side door.

Over her shoulder, she managed, "Goodbye, Maggie. I'm sorry. Maybe we can have our talk another time."

Maggie nodded and suppressed a shudder of dread. "Another time," she agreed. "Goodbye," and hoped she never saw her again. But of course she would; Maggie was convinced of that.

As the door closed she heard Wade demand, "What were you going to talk to Maggie about?"

She didn't hear Belinda's reply, but she knew the answer. Their little tiff would work itself out; Belinda would see to it.

There was no doubt in Maggie's mind that Wade had chosen his fiancée.

A remark he had made when he first walked in had given his decision away.

He had said that when he hadn't found Belinda at home, he had wondered where she was. So he had obviously been returning to her.

A broken sigh came from her heart, and her fingers raked into her tousled red hair to support her lowered head.

Being prepared for his decision didn't make the wrenching pain any easier to accept. The rest of her life yawned emptily before her and Maggie wondered how she would make it alone.

She squeezed her eyes tightly shut and bit into her lower lip.

Car doors slammed and engines started. Sniffing back a

sob, Maggie tossed her head to shake away the throes of self-pity.

Mike could walk in at any minute and she didn't want him to find her crying. There would be plenty of lonely hours to indulge in that.

CHAPTER SEVENTEEN

BRISKLY SHE ROSE to clear the coffee cups and juice glass from the table.

Returning the sugar bowl and cream to their respective places, she wiped the table and refilled her cup with coffee.

As she was walking back to the table, the side door opened.

When she saw Wade enter the kitchen, Maggie dropped the cup in her hand. It shattered on impact, spilling its hot contents on the floor amid the fragments of broken pottery.

"Damn, look what you made me do!" she cried angrily to hide the leaping joy of hope in her heart. "Do you have to burst in on people all the time? Why can't you ever knock?"

As she stooped to pick up the broken pieces, Wade was there to help.

"Be careful or you'll cut yourself," he muttered impatiently. "Let me do it. You get a rag to mop up the coffee."

Finding his closeness too disturbing, Maggie obeyed.

She took a rag from under the sink and began mopping up the floor, careful to avoid the fragments Wade hadn't collected yet.

"I thought you'd left with Belinda," she murmured to explain her shock when he had returned to the house. "I heard your car."

"I was parked behind her. I had to move my car so she could get out."

He put the broken pieces of the coffee cup in the waste bin.

"You could have gone with her. You didn't have to come back."

Maggie wished he hadn't.

"I didn't?"

A dark eyebrow lifted quizzically.

"No."

She refused to meet his look. "I realized that you'd made your decision. You didn't have to come back to tell me or explain."

"You're as bad as Belinda about jumping to conclusions," he said.

There was an underlying grimness to his voice.

Maggie thought she understood the reason for it. "Look, I know you're upset with Belinda right now. But she's young and she's trying very hard to behave the way she thinks best."

"You think I've decided to go ahead with my plans to marry Belinda?"

"Yes—you said . . . ."

Maggie made the mistake of glancing at him, and the look in his eyes confused her.

"What did I say?" Wade prompted, still watching her in that bemused way.

"Where were you last night?" she asked instead of answering.

Belinda might have been reluctant to ask him, but Maggie wasn't.

"Driving. Thinking. I drank a lot of coffee at a lot of different restaurants—I don't remember which ones."

"This morning you went to Belinda's home to see her. You said so," she reminded him.

"So you assumed that meant I was returning to her." Wade followed her comment to the conclusion Maggie had reached.

"Weren't you?" she asked, suddenly breathless.

"No, I was trying to do the proper thing. I wanted to break my engagement to her before coming to you."

He took the wet rag from her hand and tossed it in the sink.

"I never dreamed she was here."

"Are you sure?"

Maggie hardly dared to believe him. "What happened this morning didn't have anything to do with your decision?"

"It eliminated any doubts that might have been lingering."

His hands gently settled on her shoulders.

"Belinda is very understanding. I doubt if she ever loses her temper or starts arguments."

Maggie felt bound to point out the sharp contrast between them.

"Milk toast can make one feel better for a while, but a steady diet of it would soon make life very bland. Life with you was never dull, Maggie.

"I much prefer the road ahead of me to be filled with challenge. How about you?"

"Yes."

Maggie gravitated toward him. In the next second she was wrapped in the hard circle of his arms, his mouth crushing down on hers.

Joy burst from her like an eternal fountain, her happiness spilling over in the wild rush to give him all of her love. It was impossible. It would take a lifetime to do that.

Wade seemed to recognize that, too. He broke off the kiss to bury his face in the lustrous thickness of her red gold hair.

His arms remained locked around her, and she felt the powerful tremors that shuddered through him.

"I love you, Maggie." The deep intensity of his emotion couldn't be muffled.

"I pretended I didn't, even to myself. But I never stopped loving you."

"And I never stopped loving you, but I was too scared to admit it," she responded.

"You? Scared?" Wade laughed softly at the thought. "My tigress has never been afraid to tackle anything."

"That isn't true, because I was always afraid of you. I realized that last night after you'd left." Her fingers outlined the angle of his jaw, free at last to caress him as much as she wanted.

Wade lifted his head to look at her, a frown creasing his forehead.

"Why should you be afraid of me?"

Her dimples came into play for a moment. "Whether you're aware of it or not, there's a certain quality about you that's dominating. But I don't think I was so much afraid of that.

"Subconsciously I realized that I loved you so much

nothing else mattered. I was in danger of becoming totally absorbed in your personality, losing my own identity.

"I was constantly fighting that, which meant always arguing with you."

"Now?"

"Now I'm going to stop fighting the fact that I love you," Maggie promised, rising on tiptoe to kiss him.

His gaze roamed possessively over her face, the hands on her back keeping her close.

Faint, loving amusement glittered in the jet blackness of his eyes.

"Does that mean no more arguments?" he mocked.

"I doubt it," she laughed. "I'd hate to start boring you."

"I'd probably start picking fights if you did." His mouth teased the edges of her lips. "If only to have the fun of making up afterward."

CHAPTER EIGHTEEN

WHEN MAGGIE COULD no longer stand the tantalizing brush of his mouth, she sought the heady excitement of his kiss.

Wade let her take the initiative for a few breathless moments before taking over with a mastery that left her weak at the knees.

She clung to him, her heart beating wildly, as Wade forced her head back to explore the hollow at the base of her throat.

"Poor Belinda," murmured Maggie. "She's going to feel so badly when you tell her."

"I already have," he said against her skin.

"You have?"

"Yes, when I walked her to her car."

In the unending circle of his love, Maggie was generous enough to feel sympathy.

"Was she very upset?"

"Belinda?" said Wade as if it were impossible. "She took the news with her usual calmness."

"Don't tell me!" Maggie swallowed back a disbelieving laugh. "She didn't recite some platitude that it was better you found out before you married her, did she?"

"You took the words right out of her mouth," he admitted.

"She should be on exhibit in some museum. Sometimes I can't believe she's for real," she sighed.

"Belinda has a lot to learn about life and people. It's easy to think you have all the answers when you're young."

"Yes," Maggie agreed. "I'm just glad, though, that we have a second chance."

"Our marriage will be better this time," Wade promised her.

"Our heads may be in the clouds, but our feet are solidly on the ground.

"Speaking of marriage, when do you want the wedding? Is next week too soon?"

"Tomorrow couldn't be too soon," she declared.

"For me, either."

His arms tightened to crush her ribs.

"Dad?"

Mike's voice called from the living room.

The front door was closed and the sound of running feet approached the kitchen.

Maggie and Wade exchanged a smile as he burst in on them.

"I didn't know you were here, dad, until I saw the car in the driveway." His dark eyes rounded as he took in the fact that his mother was firmly enwrapped in his father's arms.

He seemed hesitant to draw any conclusion. "You aren't mad at mom anymore, are you?" was the closest he would come.

"No, I'm not mad at her anymore." Wade smiled down on Maggie, then bent his head to kiss the tip of her nose.

"By the way, Mike, I've decided I'm not going to marry Belinda."

"You're not?" he repeated uncertainly.

"No, I'm not. I've decided your mother is much more in need of a man to look after her and keep her out of trouble. I've volunteered for the job, having had past experience. And she's accepted."

"Does that mean . . ." Mike began. "Are you and mom going to get married again?"

"Yes, we are," Maggie answered.

"For good?" Mike asked.

Wade answered, "For good . . . and bad, fighting and arguing and loving for the rest of our life." He looked at Maggie as he spoke, warming every inch of her with the love that shone in his eyes. "I hope you're as happy about it as we are, Mike."

"You bet I am!" he exclaimed now that he was fully convinced that they meant it.

"Oh, wow! I hoped—does this mean we're going to live in Alaska?"

"Yes. Would like that?" Wade watched closely for Mike's reaction.

"Would I? You could teach me how to ski! And maybe we could buy a sled and some dogs? And mom could go fishing with us and catch one of those big fish like we did!"

Mike began making plans.

"With our luck, the fish will probably pull her into the water," Wade laughed.

"Wow! I gotta go tell Denny we're moving to Alaska!" Mike exclaimed, and shot out of the kitchen for the neighbor's house.

As the door banged shut behind him, Wade curved a finger under Maggie's chin and turned her head to look at him.

There was a shimmer of tears in her eyes.

"What's the matter, honey?"

"Mike was so happy." She smiled at being so silly as to cry over that.

"I know."

He gently wiped the glistening tears from her lashes. "I never did ask you whether you wanted to live in Alaska."

"You know I don't care where I live so long as it's with you," Maggie told him.

"Careful! You're beginning to sound corny," Wade teased her.

"I don't care," she sighed, and rested her head against his shoulder.

She had never known such contentment.

"We'll call the real estate company on Monday and put the house up for sale. What about the furniture? Do you want to store it or take it with us?"

"We can take some of it and store the rest," Maggie decided, and sighed.

"What's that for?"

"I was just thinking about all the packing and sorting that has to be done. I have to give notice at my job. There's the utilities to call—there's so much to do."

"Would you rather not move?" Wade asked.

"No, it's not that. I just wished I had a genie who would do it all for me."

She laughed at her laziness. "How soon will we be going?"

"After our honeymoon."

"Are we going to have a honeymoon?"

"Don't all newlyweds?" he teased.

"Where are we going?"

Maggie was curious.

"I thought we'd take the boat and go up to the San Juan Islands in the sound, maybe all the way to Vancouver," Wade told her.

"What boat? You don't mean Belinda's?"

Maggie pulled away from his arms, astounded by his suggestion. "Isn't that expecting rather a lot from her?"

"That wasn't Belinda's boat. Did you think it belonged to her family?" he queried in amusement.

"Yes. Whose else would it be? I mean, you'd borrowed her car, so I naturally assumed you'd borrowed her boat."

"Well, I didn't. It belongs to one of the men who works with me.

"He gave me the keys and told me to use it while I was here," Wade explained.

"Oh."

"Do you feel better now?" He gently drew her back into his arms.

"Much better. I'm not as open-minded as Belinda," Maggie warned him.

"The thought of spending my second honeymoon in her family's boat—"

"—touched a spark to your temper?" Wade finished the sentence for her.

"Something like that," she admitted.

"It's fitting, isn't it?"

"What?"

"For us to be leaving Seattle for Alaska, the same way the prospectors did, using this place as the jumping-off point on their way to the goldfields."

"I suppose so, except we aren't going to find gold."

"No. The only gold I'm interested in is a plain hollow circle to go around your finger." Wade found her left hand carried it up to kiss her ring finger. Then he glanced at the bareness of it. "What did you do with your rings?"

"Don't ask." Maggie shook her head and tried to withdraw her hand from his hold. "It's better if you don't know."

"Why? What *did* you do with them?" Her answer had fully aroused his curiosity.

Maggie knew he wouldn't leave the subject alone until she answered him. "I threw them in the river."

CHAPTER NINETEEN

"YOU DID *WHAT?*" Disbelieving anger darkened his eyes.

"You threw your wedding band *and* your diamond ring in the river?"

"I told you it would be better if you didn't know," she reminded him of her warning.

"Why on earth would you do that?" he demanded.

"I was mad. That day you left for Alaska, you brought Mike home, but you never came in to say goodbye to me.

"The next day I was at my lunch break. There was the river and there were the rings on my fingers. I decided if you didn't think enough of me to say goodbye, I didn't think enough of you to wear your rings. So I took them off and threw them in the river."

"Oh, Maggie!"

His anger dissipated into a rueful smile. "I didn't come in to say goodbye because I knew I'd never be able to go if I did. It wasn't because I didn't want to see you. I couldn't."

"We must be the most stubborn people in the world. Neither one of us wanted to be the first to admit we'd made a mistake about the divorce."

"It's a communication problem that isn't going to happen again. I love you, Maggie. Whatever else I say, for whatever reason, always remember that," he ordered.

"Yes, sir," she agreed with mock obedience.

"You're being impertinent!"

"You'd better do something about it," she suggested. "Try a little communication."

"We're going to have a lot of communication, but first there's a problem that needs immediate attention."

"Oh? What is that?"

Maggie challenged the thought that anything could be important.

"A place to stay. I can't very well stay at Belinda's home now that I've broken the engagement."

"That is a problem," Maggie agreed. "I guess you could always move in here. You can always sleep on the couch."

"The couch, hell!" he growled against her lips.

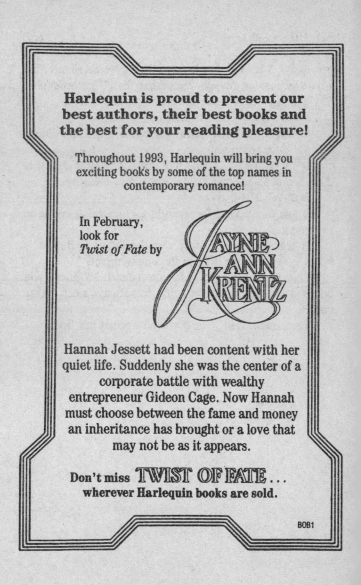

HARLEQUIN®

my Valentine 1993

The most romantic day of the year is here! Escape into the exquisite world of love with MY VALENTINE 1993. What better way to celebrate Valentine's Day than with this very romantic, sensuous collection of four original short stories, written by some of Harlequin's most popular authors.

**ANNE STUART
JUDITH ARNOLD
ANNE McALLISTER
LINDA RANDALL WISDOM**

**THIS VALENTINE'S DAY, DISCOVER ROMANCE
WITH MY VALENTINE 1993**

WELCOME TO

**The quintessential small town,
where everyone knows everybody else!**

Each book set in Tyler is a self-contained love story; together,
the twelve novels stitch the fabric of the community.

"The small town warmth and friendliness shine through."
Rendezvous

Join your friends in Tyler for the twelfth book,
LOVEKNOT by Marisa Carroll, available in February.

*Does Alyssa Baron really hold the key to Margaret's death?
Will Alyssa and Edward consummate the romance they began more than
thirty years ago?*

GREAT READING...GREAT SAVINGS...AND A
FABULOUS FREE GIFT!

With Tyler you can receive a fabulous gift, ABSOLUTELY FREE,
by collecting proofs-of-purchase found in each Tyler book.
And use our special Tyler coupons to save on your next
TYLER book purchase.

If you missed *Whirlwind* (March), *Bright Hopes* (April), *Wisconsin Wedding* (May), *Monkey Wrench* (June), *Blazing Star* (July), *Sunshine* (August), *Arrowpoint* (September), *Bachelor's Puzzle* (October), *Milky Way* (November), *Crossroads* (December) or *Courthouse Steps* (January) and would like to order them, send your name, address, zip or postal code, along with a check or money order for $3.99 for each book ordered (please do not send cash), plus 75¢ postage and handling ($1.00 in Canada), payable to Harlequin Reader Service, to:

In the U.S.

3010 Walden Avenue
P.O. Box 1325
Buffalo, NY 14269-1325

In Canada

P.O. Box 609
Fort Erie, Ontario
L2A 5X3

Please specify book title(s) with your order.
Canadian residents add applicable federal and provincial taxes.

TYLER-12

Crystal Creek

COME FOR A VISIT—TEXAS-STYLE!

Where do you find hot Texas nights, smooth Texas charm and dangerously sexy cowboys? CRYSTAL CREEK!

This March, join us for a year in Crystal Creek...where power and influence live in the land, and in the hands of one family determined to nourish old Texas fortunes and to forge new Texas futures.

CRYSTAL CREEK reverberates with the exciting rhythm of Texas. Each story features the rugged individuals who live and love in the Lone Star State. And each one ends with the same invitation...

Y'ALL COME BACK...REAL SOON!

Watch for this exciting saga of a unique Texas family in March, wherever Harlequin Books are sold.

CC-G

 HARLEQUIN®

ROMANCE IS A YEARLONG EVENT!

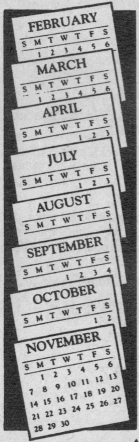

Celebrate the most romantic day of the year with MY VALENTINE! (February)

CRYSTAL CREEK
When you come for a visit Texas-style, you won't want to leave! (March)

Celebrate the joy, excitement and adjustment that comes with being JUST MARRIED! (April)

Go back in time and discover the West as it was meant to be . . . UNTAMED— Maverick Hearts! (July)

LINGERING SHADOWS
New York Times bestselling author Penny Jordan brings you her latest blockbuster. Don't miss it! (August)

BACK BY POPULAR DEMAND!!!
Calloway Corners, involving stories of four sisters coping with family, business and romance! (September)

FRIENDS, FAMILIES, LOVERS
Join us for these heartwarming love stories that evoke memories of family and friends. (October)

Capture the magic and romance of Christmas past with HARLEQUIN HISTORICAL CHRISTMAS STORIES! (November)

WATCH FOR FURTHER DETAILS IN ALL HARLEQUIN BOOKS!